THE DEVIL'S LAIRD

BRENDA JERNIGAN
AWARD WINNING AUTHOR

DEDICATION

This book is for all my readers who always want more and are patient enough to wait until I get the books done.

And for my twin granddaughters Olive and June. I love you.

And for my husband who asked me to write this book years ago. I love you more today than yesterday.

Special thanks to my friend Sue-Ellen Welfonder who kept telling me to get the book done. Thanks for all your help. I wouldn't have gotten the book finished without you.

EXCERPT

He could still taste the stench of burning wood and see the women's bodies in his mind's eye. He had to step over them, searching . . . searching until he found Gillian, her face so swollen he'd barely knew her.

He had blamed himself for not leaving enough men to properly protect his holding that day. Frantically, he had searched for his son. When he couldn't find him, he had found a banner from Fidach, and knew who was responsible. Roderick's men had lost loved ones, as well, and the mood was grim as they began to bury their dead. As dusk fell, Roderick had vowed they would rebuild the holding as it was before. This time they would paint the walls black so all who saw would remember this terrible day.

His boy, four-year-old Michael had never been found. Roderick had hoped to question Fidach as to what happened to his son before killing the man, but now that opportunity was lost. Somehow, he couldn't bury the past completely. He couldn't see a small child surviving alone, but he still held hope that one day he would find his son alive.

PRAISE FOR BRENDA JERNIGAN

Brenda's books have been a finalist
Booksellers Best Award
Holt Medallion Award
Maggie Award

"Ms. Jernigan writes adventure and magic."
Publishers Weekly

"Ms. Jernigan takes an old plot and makes it fresh and exciting."
Rendezvous Magazine

"Ms. Jernigan writes her stories with a true flair for love and
romance." A Romance Review

"Tender love story with a feisty heroine, a rugged hero and
charming children. Don't miss it!" Joan Johnston - NY Times
Bestselling Author

"A passionate, witty, delightful read...filled with snappy
dialogue and great characters. I couldn't put it down. A definite
keeper." Fiona Hood-Steward

"As usual her characters are interesting, her plot action-packed,
and her love story filled with conflict and emotion. A great read
from a talented writer." Rendezvous Magazine

"Cassie Edwards' readers are sure to find Brenda Jernigan irresistible ..." Rhapsody Debut Author - Rhapsody Book Club

"Brenda Jernigan has written an emotionally touching novel that tugs the heartstrings in all the right ways. I fell in love with all the characters. This is truly a fantastic read that should be savored and enjoyed over and over again. I look forward to many more books from this wonderful author." Interludes Magazine

"Don't start this one until you are sure you will have plenty of time to read. You won't want to put it down. AWESOME! Highly recommended!" Huntress Reviews

PRAISE FOR THE DEVIL'S LAIRD

"Outstanding! Jernigan delights with her special brand of romance and adventure, this time adding the danger and excitement of medieval Scotland, along with just enough magic to thrill fans of the genre. The Devil's Laird is a keeper."
~ Sue-Ellen Welfonder, USA Today Bestselling Author of award-winning Devil in a Kilt

"I couldn't get enough of Roderick and Siena's story. A page-turner from beginning to end! Fleshed out, wonderful characters that had me rooting for them from page one!"
~Paula Quinn, NYT Bestselling Author & USA Today Bestselling Author of **Forbidden Heart.**

"Historical romance at its best! Brenda Jernigan's The Devil's Laird is a must read if you love medieval Scotland!"
~New York Times Bestselling Author Lori Handeland Author of Just Once

"Jernigan sweeps you away into breathtaking settings, magical plots, multi-dimensional characters, brilliant dialogue with swoon worthy saviors, and a heroine with a magical heart! This includes sizzling hot passionate love scenes that absolutely makes your pulse race and temperature rise! An enchanting novel that I absolutely loved!"

~ **Barb Massabrook – The Tartan Book Reviews**

"Loved it! Lots of action, Highland justice, a hunky laird, magic and a love story….what more could you want? The villains are despicable, the servants are loyal and some of the clansmen are a hoot. This book starts off at a run and doesn't stop until the last page. If you like Scottish romances, you will definitely want to read this story."

~**Jayne Butcher – Goodreads 5 stars**

"This is a highlander book I never knew I needed but now cannot live without. I feel down the historical romance genre this summer and love highlander books the best. The story between Siena and Roderick is wonderful, you feel the pull on both sides, and that there are hints of legend and lore is just the icing on the cake. I just finished reading this and don't want to give away any spoilers but know that this is a wonderful story come to life and I can't wait to read by Ms. Jernigan. I couldn't put it down and read it in one night."

~**Alisue – Goodreads – 5 stars**

"I can't say enough about this fantastic book. I was sucked into the action and drama from the very first page. I loved Siena so much she had so much to learn about herself, she also would do all in her power for others. Roderick was a larger-than-life character and I think he was awesome. I couldn't stop reading till the end. I wanted more."

~Loreli Jessee – Goodreads 5 stars

AUTHOR'S NOTE

Yes, I know it has taken 4 years to release this book. I never said I was quick. :) But I am hoping that you will find the book was worth the 4 year wait.

I tend to get unorganized. I can never find my research notes and even though I have several notebooks full of research - my notes are never where I think they are.

I thought you'd enjoy seeing my orange folder for this book, and you can see by the writing on the front what I'm talking about. I think I have taped the folder together at least 10 times.

Also on bad days, the floor becomes my workspace. :)

A note to readers - The Green Woman's name is spelled Elen with one l not two.

If you would like to see a picture of the stones - they are in the back of the book. They have been on my desk the entire time. Until then … let your imagination carry you away.

CHAPTER 1

From the land of mists and waters she came....

Berwick Castle
    Northumbria, England
    Medieval England & Scotland

They were going to hang her.

And the strange part . . . she really didn't care.

Fidach, had beaten her for the last time.

Lady Siena Bertram had had all she was going to take from her brother. When he'd lunged at her she'd had no choice but to stab him through his black heart. Aye, she regretted taking a life, but when the life was that of a snake, Siena hoped God would forgive her.

Evidently, Fidach's men didn't agree . . . since they were the ones who intended to hang her.

Siena's body ached all over from the beating her brother had inflicted upon her, and now the rough handling by his men, who were treating her like a criminal instead of a lady, wasn't helping. Blood trickled from the side of her mouth.

There was a gash on her arm that needed tending, and she could feel her face swelling. Since a noose dangled in front of her, she supposed a cut wasn't the worst of her problems, and that simple thought made her smile. Now she wondered if she were truly daft. Who would smile when they were getting ready to hang?

Glancing around at the gathered crowd in the bailey, Siena thought she would have had some support from her own people. A few did look uncomfortable, especially the ones she'd healed in the past, but what could they do? Mostly they stood helplessly watching and doing nothing to stop the hanging. Did they, too, think she was a witch?

Twisting her wrists, she tried to alleviate the pressure of the rough ropes that bound her, realizing she'd been cursed from the day she was born. She had heard the gossip. They said she'd sucked the breath from her twin brother, so she might live. Of course, that was utterly absurd. However, the strange birthmark on her wrist, which resembled a pitchfork, only added fuel to the gossip-mongers.

The only blessing that Siena possessed was the vision of sight. However, it didn't always work, or she would surely have seen this noose being slipped over her head. The guard tightened the noose, placing the knot behind her left ear. She flinched at the pressure on her throat.

She grew tired of not belonging.

Perhaps, death would be better.

And then she saw *him*…the devil, face painted blue, charging toward her on a huge black beast.

She was going to hell for sure.

They said he made a deal with the Devil….

On the hilltop overlooking Berwick Castle, Laird Roderick Scott threw up his right hand and pulled Hercules, his black destrier, to a halt. His face was painted blue and he was breathing hard. How long had he waited for this day?

A day to right a wrong … a day to avenge his family's death.

The rest of his men halted behind him except, Duncan, Roderick's first in command, who rode up beside him and asked, "What do ye make of it?"

Roderick leaned forward on his pommel. "Does it not strike ye as odd that no one seems to be guardin' the castle and the drawbridge is down?"

Duncan nodded. "Aye. The battlements look bare. Almost as if no one is home." He watched Roderick and noted the scowl on his laird's face. *The mon was no' happy*, Duncan thought, and he pitied any man who got in his way today.

"Could be a trap," Roderick said, shifting in his saddle. "I canna imagine Fidach has been tipped off we were comin'."

"I can see smoke coming from the chimneys, so the bastards

3

are there." When Roderick remained quiet, Duncan asked, "What say ye? We dinna put on war paint for nothin'."

"Take all the men but three around the back of the castle, and I'll take the others with me through the main gate. I want Fidach to ken I'm coming for him. Remember, Fidach is to be caught alive. He dies by my hand."

"As he should," Duncan said, and motioned the men forward. Roderick waited until the group had made their way to the back of the castle, then he and the rest of his men started down the hill.

On this cold, January morning, the crisp air blew around them and felt good on his face as they rode. They galloped down the bottom half of the hill, across the drawbridge, and straight into the enemy's castle without one arrow being shot.

Surprise would be on his side.

However, Roderick wasn't prepared for the chaos he saw once they rode through the entrance. There was no one manning the main gate. The entire castle seemed to be out in the bailey. Small fires burned here and there, giving off rotten smells so that the smoke made the air hazy. Everyone, including the castle guards, who had their backs toward the main gate, were gathered on the left side of the bailey near a raised wooden platform.

It appeared they were preparing to hang someone.

Roderick nudged his mount and they moved closer, so he could get a better view. The crowd parted for him, but no one paid him any attention or his men. Instead, their attention was on the hangman. As Roderick drew near, he saw long, black hair hanging over the noose. My God, they were hanging a woman! What in God's name could they be thinking?

A big, burly guard was getting ready to shove the stool out

from under the lass. As he kicked at the stool, Roderick charged forward, parting the rest of the crowd by knocking them down. Just in time, he reached the girl and snatched her up just as she lost her footing. The hangman had fallen backward in his haste to get away from the rider, and his body had loosened the rope that he'd never gotten secured.

Roderick jerked the woman into his arms before the rope could break her neck, then settled her on his lap in front of him. His men moved to flank him for protection. Gently, he loosened the noose and pulled it over her head, noticing the rope burns on her neck. Next, he removed the ropes from her wrists, yet she still hung limp against his chest. Was he too late? Roderick leaned down and placed two fingers on the side of her neck. A slight thumping beneath his fingertips, gave him his answer.

She lived!

Slowly, he let out the breath he hadn't realized he'd been holding.

The girl's clothes were torn and stained with blood. A four-inch gash on her arm was bleeding, and her lip and one eye were swollen and turning blue. To add to that, she now had rope burns around her neck. The woman had been through hell this day. It was probably a blessing she was unconscious.

The men-at-arms, having noticed that they were no longer alone, had drawn their swords. They appeared ready to fight off the intruders.

The fools!

Roderick thought as he insolently studied the soldiers from his position high upon Hercules, daring them to give him a reason to murder the lot. Rage ran hot in his veins; Roderick took a deep breath and waited for his temper to cool.

Everyone need not die because of a few fools.

After a moment, he gave them a contemptuous smile. "Where is Fidach, son of Cinge?" Roderick bellowed so that his voice carried over the crowd's noise as Hercules pranced beneath him. Roderick tightened his knees and the horse settled down.

One of Fidach's soldiers approached and spat on the ground. "Who the bloody hell are you?"

Roderick's temper flared again. Since he still held the woman, he couldn't very well throw her on the ground and challenge the insolent guard, so he bumped the man with his stallion, knocking him flat on his back. The rest of the castle guards rushed to surround him, their swords raised ready for battle. However, they kept their distance, afraid of the big black horse who stood twenty hands tall. He was snorting and stomping his hooves and appeared just as mean as the man who rode him.

"W--what business do you have with Fidach?" the man stammered, having seen the cold fury in Roderick's eyes.

"That would be between Fidach and myself," Roderick replied lazily.

A guard in the back of the group yelled, "Drag him off his horse! There are only four of them." The man closest lunged, but Roderick was fast, drawing his short sword with his left hand he sliced the man's sword arm. The scream of agony echoed around the compound, gaining the rest of men's attention.

"I would look around--" Roderick suggested as his horse pawed the ground. He paused to allow his words to sink in, then he tightened his reins; even Hercules was anxious for battle. "-- before you try anything foolish."

The castle guards glanced up at the battlements to find Roderick's men had surrounded them. One of the castle guards dropped his sword, then another and another.

The men on the battlements shouted, "A Bellendaine!"

"What the bloody hell does that mean?" a guard on the ground grumbled.

"It means ... the Scotts are out!" Roderick said in his Scottish burr. "I repeat," he ground out even louder, his temper growing short. "Where is yer lord?"

"Dead," spat the guard closest to him. "She—" He pointed to the girl in Roderick's arms "—she killed him, she did! Lady Siena is possessed. She sees things others do not."

"This is yer lady?" Roderick asked, dumbfounded by the way she'd been treated by her own people.

The crowd murmured and nodded their agreement.

"Then why do ye not protect her?"

"Her brother said she was cursed from the day she was born." A woman in the crowd, most likely a servant from the way she was dressed, called out, "Bad blood."

"There is no such thing." Roderick frowned. He didn't believe in curses. Glancing down, he saw nothing wrong with the girl other than she'd been abused. Her long, black hair fell away from a petite face . . . or it would be once the swelling went down. He feared for her safety if she stayed here.

He leveled his gaze back on the men and women and waited until all eyes were directed his way. Some looked annoyed, others slightly frightened. "Hear me and hear me well . . . I am Laird Roderick Scott, Warlord of Kirkurd. I proclaim this castle is now mine!" He paused and waited for his words to sink in. He heard the murmur of *The Devil's Laird*. A name he'd been often called.

The rest of Fidach's men lowered their weapons. He saw the fright in their eyes that his reputation always produced. "I'll leave a few of my men with you. If ye canna pledge allegiance to me, then ye'er free to walk out the gate by sundown. After that, my men will show ye no mercy."

It only took seconds before shouts went out, "Laird Scott! Laird Scott!" echoed through the crowd.

Roderick heard his name on everyone's lips as they backed away to give him plenty of room. He wasn't sure how he felt. It had been over a year since he had sworn vengeance against Fidach. Now justice had been done; yet he felt no satisfaction. Perhaps, it was because he'd not been the one to end the miserable cur's life. He owed that deed to the girl. And that made one more reason he'd not leave her here to die.

Roderick made his way to the stone steps of the great hall. There he instructed his men what he wanted done. From the looks of disrepair around him, there was much work ahead of them. He'd take five of his best men back with him to his holding, they would be enough to provide a safe journey, but the rest would remain here. His army would grow with the capture of Berwick, which was on the English border but now his. It would take time to shape these men into what he wanted, after all, he was known for training the best men in Scotland.

Duncan pulled his mount up next to Roderick and asked, "What of the woman?"

Roderick jerked his head toward his first in command, but before he could answer, an older woman, heavyset and square-jawed, with gray-streaked, brown hair rushed through the door, and down the steps of the great hall.

"Is she alive?" The woman cried out as she scuttled over to his horse, where she placed a hand upon the girl. He got the impression the woman didn't care if he was here to kill everyone in the castle as long as he protected the one he held. He also noticed her face showed bruises like those of her mistress.

"Aye, but barely," he finally said. "I take it ye know this woman?"

She nodded but didn't look up at him. "I am Lady Siena's maid, sire." The servant answered hastily, then continued, "I have been with Siena since the day she was born, and I can tell you she is not safe here."

"Why is that?"

The woman placed both her hands on her ample hips. "Her good-for-nothing brother convinced everyone in the holding that Siena is possessed. It's because of Fidach that they do not trust her." She waved a hand in the air. "Can they not see how she has been mistreated? Her brother should have been killed long before now," she finished, and then muttered under her breath. "We'd all have been better off."

He nodded toward the girl. "So Fidach did this to her?"

"Aye."

Roderick took a deep breath. He wished the son of a bitch were still alive so he could beat him to a bloody pulp before killing him again. Finally, he asked, "Yer name?"

At last, Agatha managed to look at the warrior on the great beast and she had to catch her breath. Good Lord Almighty, the man was huge with broad shoulders and his eyes were dark and cold, so that she felt like he was looking through her. He wasn't bad to gaze upon if she could only stop shaking. "M--my name is Agatha, sire." She curtsied, clumsily. "I beg you, protect Lady Siena and take her away with you."

"You and I agree on one thing . . . Fidach should have died

sooner," Roderick said with a nod. Agatha smiled, and he knew right away he liked something about her. She had an honest face and he saw kindness also. He studied her for a moment, then commanded, "Go and pack for yer lady and yourself. You will be returnin' with us."

Once Agatha had scurried off to do his bidding, Roderick told Duncan, "Give me something to wrap around the lass's arm, or she'll be dead by the time we camp tonight."

Duncan produced a long strip of clean cloth to wrap the woman's arm. He agreed. The cut was a nasty wound indeed, so he poured whisky over it, then wrapped the cloth around her arm. Duncan wondered at the odd behavior of his leader. Why hadn't Roderick handed the girl to one of his men, so his hands would be free? It was almost like he was protecting her. The woman was definitely in bad shape, and Duncan couldn't call her pretty with her swollen eye and a fat lip, but it was the first time in a long while that Roderick had shown any interest in a woman. Nonetheless, Duncan would not question his leader. He knew of Roderick's temper. He wasn't one to be crossed.

Roderick turned his horse, so he was facing the crowd. He waited as one by one the people approached him and pledged their allegiance to him. When all had finished, Duncan reported that five soldiers had left the castle.

"That is their choice," Roderick said. "Bring three horses from the stables around here."

"Three?"

"Is it not what I said?" Roderick asked with a frown. He wasn't used to explaining his actions, but to get Duncan moving he added, "Lady Siena and her lady's maid plus an extra horse for their belongs. They will be accompanying us back to our holding."

He saw Duncan raise his brow to question bringing the lasses with them; however, he knew better and once again held his tongue. Roderick couldn't explain why he'd chosen to take this woman with him, other than he wanted to protect her, which made no sense at all.

He picked five of his most stalwart men to ride with him, and a short time later they were ready to leave. He instructed Gareth and Maclean to strap the bags, which Agatha had packed onto the extra horse. After giving final instructions to Gordon for securing the castle, Roderick and his men began their journey back to Black Dawn.

"Fergus take the lead," Roderick commanded as they crossed the drawbridge.

The weather was brisk, but their speed was good as they traveled across the rolling countryside. He didn't much like riding out in the open and would feel better once they passed over the Cheviot Hills up to higher ground. They had ridden only a few hours, when Duncan rode up beside Roderick. "Are ye certain the lass is alive?" Duncan asked.

Roderick glanced down at the warm body held next to his chest. "Aye."

"What are ye going to do with her?"

"Truth be told. I've not given it much thought. I couldna leave her behind for fear of her safety, and..." he paused. "Then there is the small fact she did kill our enemy for me. Even though, I'd rather have killed him myself." He sighed with regret that he hadn't been the one to end Fidach's life. "I owe the lass somethin'. I've no doubt that she'll fit into our household."

"But she is a lady," Duncan protested.

"Aye. Though at the moment she looks no better than a servant."

Duncan nodded. "Do ye want me to take her for a while and give yer arm a rest?"

Roderick glanced at the battered woman nestled in his arms. "Nay. The sun is going down. We'll camp for tonight and give the horses a rest. She'll be waking soon."

"Gareth!" Roderick called, then waited for him to join them. "Find a suitable place to make camp."

Without warning, the slip of a girl in Roderick's arms bolted straight up, bumping his chin. He had to tighten his hold to keep her from falling. The sudden shifting on Hercules's back, startled the horse, and he reared. Roderick tightened his knees to keep them both seated.

"By all that is holy! Hold still before we both fall to our deaths!"

CHAPTER 2

The woman squirmed and struck him several times until he wrapped his arms tighter around her, pinning her arms against her sides. His patience had worn thin. "Och, get still or I swear, lass, I'll toss ye on the ground myself."

Roderick realized that the woman had no idea who he was, so he took a calming breath. "I'll no hurt ye, lass. I'm not one of yer brother's men. Stop fightin' me." Roderick saw uncertainty in one wild, blue eye as the other was swollen. "I'm the one who pulled ye from the hangman's noose." Patience wasn't something he possessed in great quantities and this slip of a girl was trying his patience greatly.

"For Christ's sake, lass. If I had wanted to harm ye, I'd have left ye to dangle from the end of a rope," he said, frustrated. "And I'm beginnin' to doubt the mercy I've shown ye." This woman was going to be more trouble than she was worth, he'd wager. "I'll loosen my grip if ye will hold still."

He glared down at her and in a stern voice said, "I'll have yer promise now."

Agatha rode up beside them and laid a weathered hand gently on Siena's arm. "Milady, he is helping us. It will be all right."

"He is blue! He's the devil."

"Nay. He has on warpaint and that is the reason he is blue, milady," Agatha explained.

At long last the girl relaxed at the sight of her maid, then croaked, "Some water, please."

"In a minute," Roderick told her.

Warily, Siena watched the warrior who held her, wondering how she'd gotten in this position when she should have been dangling at the end of a rope.

She remembered seeing a man on a black horse coming through the crowd just before the stool had been shoved out from beneath her feet. She thought it had been the Devil come to claim her, then she recalled her breath leaving her body, and she shuddered at the memory. By the grace of God, she'd been spared. Yet she felt her neck and found it tender to the touch. Apparently, this man had saved her. Now that everything was over, she felt his strong arms around her, and found it comforting. She had no idea why she should feel this way when men had always been trouble in her past.

The intimidating warrior was huge, and his dark eyes were penetrating. She couldn't help feeling as though he was trying to see deep inside her when he looked at her, but at the moment he wasn't paying her any attention. "Water," she rasped again. Her throat was so parched it felt like it was on fire.

At last, the man nodded and nudged his mount over to a clearing in the middle of oak trees. The dead leaves on the ground would provide a good cushion for their tired bodies when they slept.

The sun was lowering, giving a dusky glow to the clearing. Only then did Siena notice that there were five other men with them, and they were dismounting too. Who were these strangers? And why had this man saved her? Thankfully, she didn't recognize any of them. Of course, it was hard to get past their blue painted faces. They would scare the hell out of anyone.

However, her brother's solders were no better than he was, and she was grateful, but she didn't yet trust any of them. They appeared to be Scots. They wore red with green and black pinstriped plaids. The tartan pattern consisted of crisscrossed horizontal colors that came to the top of their knees. The rest of their legs were covered in doe-skinned boots. Everyone knew the Scots had no love for the English, so she wasn't sure she was any better off. She'd learned a long time ago not to trust anyone no matter if they were English or Scot.

A warrior with long, blond hair approached and shoved a soft-skinned pouch up toward her. With trembling hands, she took the pouch and lifted it to her dry lips. The cool water felt like refreshing nectar on her dry throat. "Thank you," she said as she handed the brown, leather pouch back to the man on the ground.

She turned and looked at the warrior who held her and asked, "Who are you?"

"I'm Laird Roderick Scott, Warlord of Kirkurd."

She knew the name, but her head hurt too much to think, and her right arm throbbed mercilessly. Perhaps later she could think straight. "I am Lady Siena of Berwick. I know I'm merely a captive, and I'm sure you're very busy, but my arm really hurts." She held it up and the throbbing increased. "I see a bandage. Has it been stitched?"

"Nay." Roderick didn't bother to look at her, his attention seemed drawn to his men as he added, "We'll be caring for yer arm once we make camp and get settled, lass. We need to make sure we are safe first."

Another soldier just as big as the first approached Roderick and held his arms up to help her down, she hesitated until she heard Roderick say, "We will camp here tonight." He pushed her toward the other man.

Siena felt like a sack of wool being passed around. She didn't fight this time, but allowed herself to be lifted down, not that she had much choice. The moment her feet touched the ground, her legs buckled. She grabbed the warrior's arms to keep from falling. "I--I'm so sorry. My legs have gone numb."

Roderick dismounted. Immediately, he wrapped an arm around her waist. She was surprised how gentle he could be for someone so large. "Ah, wull, ye can lean on me while my men prepare bedding for you."

Siena was thankful for his assistance. She hurt all over, and her legs tingled with what felt like a thousand needles sticking into them. She flexed her feet not caring one bit for this help-less feeling. Slowly, the stinging stopped, and she felt the blood returning to her legs so that she was able to support herself, however, the laird still had his arm around her for support.

Siena quickly glanced around. The campsite was ideal as it had a cliff behind them with tall oak trees around the clearing providing them with good protection. The cold air whipped around the cliff, causing her to shiver. She wished she had her woolen cloak.

"I—I'm grateful, sir, but still a little confused," Siena said looking up at Roderick. She almost gasped at his dark eyes. Surely, they were not black, but they definitely didn't show any emotion. "How did you come to be at Berwick?"

"I came to kill yer brother, lass," he said with very little expression. Maybe his eyes were black after all and cold. "But I found ye had saved me the trouble, so I took you instead."

"But I am worth nothing."

"I didna take ye for ransom. You did me a favor and the verra least I could do was bring ye to safety. I'm pretty sure ye were not safe at yer home."

"My brother was a true bastard," she said with a shrug, her cheeks turning pink for boldly speaking her thoughts.

Roderick gave a bark of laughter. "Of that you and I agree. Did yer brother give ye that black eye?"

She nodded. She liked the sound of his laughter. Laughter wasn't something she'd heard often in her lifetime.

"I promise ye somethin' like that willna happen to you again." He motioned toward two red plaids, woolen blankets spread across the ground. "There is yer bedding. Has the tingling stopped? Can ye walk now?"

"Aye."

"Ah wull, we will go and wash off the warpaint while you both get settled."

Agatha moved over to where they stood. "You are shivering. We're lucky Laird Scott and his men arrived when they did. He saved you from being hanged; a minute later and you would have died."

Siena followed Agatha to the pallet of blankets where they both sat down. A campfire had been built in the center of the clearing with the beds arranged all around the fire. Already she could feel the much-needed warmth from the fire. Agatha had brought a couple of wicker baskets and placed them beside her.

"I am so glad that my brother didn't kill you," Siena said with a sigh. "He told me you were dead."

"Your brother only knocked me down. I wasn't worth killing to his mind." Agatha shrugged. "Begging your pardon, milady, we are better off without him."

"I'm sure we are," Siena agreed. She opened the basket next to her, but she only saw food. "You didn't happen to bring my cloak, did you?"

"I did." Agatha reached into a soft sack and pulled out the purple cloak. "A bit wrinkled, but I'm sure it will shake out once you have it on."

"I don't care about the wrinkles. I want the warmth." Siena gratefully wrapped the cloak around her, and then glanced around at the dense forest. "Where are we going?"

"To Laird Scott's holding. Like he said, you wouldn't have been safe at Berwick, so I begged him to take us with him, or should I say myself because I was sure he was taking you." Agatha laughed. "You know, milady, he hasn't let go of you until we arrived here at the clearing and you started hitting him."

"I do recall him saying he was going to toss me to the ground." Siena smiled. "I'm glad he didn't. I'm not sure I could take many more bruises today." Her dark eyebrows slanted in a frown. "You know, I've never felt at home in Berwick. Do you suppose the Laird's castle will be any better? Will we be accepted?"

"Laird Scott seems smart, milady, and strong. His people will accept us. I'm thinking of it as a new beginning."

"His name sounds familiar but, at the moment, I cannot

place his holding. Are we not his prisoners? It would seem so since my brother was his enemy."

"I—I'm not sure, milady," Agatha said. She reached into one of the baskets and produced a couple of blankets, which she set to the side. "Lord Roderick hasn't treated us as such. I'm sure he'll take care of us. I know he appears fierce, but I don't sense the same cruelty like your brother had buried deep in him."

"Perhaps," Siena said in a not so convincing manner. She had lost everything. What man would want her now? She wasn't too sure she needed a man especially if he was like her brother. Hadn't her brother always told her how plain she was, and no man would want her? And what would she do at this other holding? She sighed. Could her life never be simple?

She wanted somebody to love her and care about her, and most of all she wanted to feel safe. Agatha was the only one who had ever taken an interest in her. Siena's mother had died with her twin brother when she was born, so she'd never had a mother's love, and her father had believed she was the cause of her mother's death.

Evidently, something was wrong with her when her own family didn't love her.

CHAPTER 3

*R*oderick stood, feet braced apart, on the other side of the fire talking with one of his men. Siena noticed that they had been to the stream to wash off their war paint, so they didn't look as scary as earlier.

There was something about his name that sounded familiar, but again, she couldn't place it. She knew she'd never seen him before because no one would forget meeting a man so large and powerful … and handsome. Aye, he was very handsome.

"Agatha, do you know the name of his holding?"

"Nay, I've not heard him say," she replied as she unpacked food, which she'd stored in one of the baskets. "You must be hungry, milady." She handed Siena a piece of chicken and a chunk of cheese.

The smell of chicken reminded Siena that she hadn't eaten since the day before. She tried not to tear into the chicken, but nibbled, remembering she was a lady, however, her swollen lip hurt when she opened her mouth, so she had to eat slow. Her arm still needed mending, but it would have to wait until she had something to eat.

"We have food if you're hungry," Siena called to the men who were now gathering around the campfire that Gareth had built. They seemed hesitant until Roderick accepted a chicken leg. The men followed his lead and fetched pieces of chicken and cheese. In turn, they handed the ladies a flask of whisky to wash down their meal. Siena noticed how the men's mood seemed lighter as they ate and talked among themselves. At least, no one was frowning at the moment, and without those frowns, they didn't look so fierce, and they were not glaring at her with hatred.

Roderick sat down near her, but he remained quiet as he ate. Siena thought he was one of the most handsome men she'd ever seen, even if he did have a ferocious look about him. He had long, dark, brown hair that was overly long and framed his face perfectly. There wasn't much about him that wasn't perfect. He seemed a true warrior and so much larger than her brother's men. His deeply tanned skin and broad shoulders proved that he attended to his training well. She felt very small sitting beside him, yet she was unafraid and that puzzled her. Siena wondered what he was thinking. She couldn't tell because there wasn't any emotion in his eyes, just a cold, hard stare. He glanced over and caught her looking at him, causing her to blush that she'd been caught in the act.

When Roderick had finished his chicken, he said, "We need to look at yer arm, lass. I had little time to examine it before we left Berwick." Siena nodded and carefully held her arm out, wincing from the pain. Roderick pulled the dirk from his boot and carefully cut the bandage with the sharp blade, so he could easily unwrap the cloth. He turned her arm as he examined it, causing her to flinch again. Evidently the man didn't know his own strength. "Och, this cut is deep, lass. Needs stitching."

"Agatha, did you bring my medicine kit?" Siena croaked.

"Aye." Agatha fumbled in the brown cloth sack until she found a small wooden box, which she handed it to Siena. "But you cannot stitch yourself, milady."

"Nay, I cannot, but you can."

Agatha started shaking her head. "I'm afraid that I would surely swoon after the first stitch, but I can thread the needle." However, after searching through the box she said, "We have no thread."

Siena looked up at Roderick. "Can you sew?"

"Probably not as well as you," he admitted then turned to one of his men. "Fergus, do ye huv yer thread and needle?"

Fergus had red hair; a bushy red beard and merry, blue eyes, though he still appeared a fierce warrior … only more inviting than the rest. She questioned that he would be doing the sewing with such big hands. Yet, she knew something had to be done.

"Aye, sire."

"Fetch it."

"But—" Agatha stopped abruptly when Roderick stared at her.

"If we dinna tend the wound, it will become infected and fester," Roderick said, cutting Agatha off. "You said ye couldna stitch the wound, but someone has to." He handed Siena a whisky flask. "Drink some of this, lass. It will help with the pain."

"Nay. You'll need that, as well." She nodded toward the flask.

"We must pour it over the wound. The dried blood will have to be cleaned off before you can sew up my arm."

"Ye've done this in the past?"

"I'm not usually the patient." Siena smiled. "I'm the one doing the sewing." She found she liked Roderick's Scottish burr. Sometimes it was thicker than other times, but it was different from her proper English. "I'll try not to scream," she paused then blurted out, "Second thought, you had better give me some whisky."

Both men chuckled.

Roderick positioned himself so that he was leaning against a tree. He spread his legs, then motioned for her to come to him. "Sit and lean against me. I'll support yer arm while Fergus does the sewing. Ye need not be scairt. He is the best I have with a needle and has stitched me more times than I care to remember."

Once Siena had settled herself against him, Roderick found an overwhelming need to protect her. Something he'd not felt in a long, long time. He believed there was something special about Siena. She seemed so small, and her bruises told him she hadn't had a pleasant life.

He also noticed the one eye he could see clearly was a silvery blue, much like a cold winter's lake. He wondered what she would look like once the swelling and bruises went away. She felt comfortable in his arms, he admitted, and her head fit just under his chin.

He watched Fergus thread the needle with horsehair. To Siena's credit, she didn't flinch, showing she had gumption. He liked that.

"This will sting a wee bit, lass," Fergus warned.

"I know," Siena whispered with an attempt at a smile.

However, her face hurt from the bruises, so she wasn't certain she'd managed one. "I have been through much this day. I believe I can take a little more pain."

"I could knock ye out, lass," Fergus said with a laugh.

"I think not, Fergus. Remember I killed the last man who hit me."

"Feisty, wee lass," Fergus chuckled. He poured more whisky over her cut, and Roderick felt her back tense, but she didn't jerk away or cry out in pain. She held her head high and bravely submitted to Fergus's ministrations. Roderick was proud of her courage. There was more to the lass than he'd thought. He sensed in her a real fighter.

He held her arm still as Fergus took the first stitch. She drew in a breath and looked away, squeezing Roderick's free hand for support. He was surprised that she turned to him for comfort as if there were already trust between them.

"Oh, my lord," Agatha gasped before she fainted and toppled over sideways on the blankets.

"S--she has a faint-heart, I'm afraid," Siena managed to say through clenched teeth.

Roderick smiled. "You, lass, are the brave one." He didn't mention she had a tight grip on his arm, so he knew she experienced a great deal of pain. He decided to take her mind off the mending of her arm. "Is Agatha related to ye?"

"Nay. My father is alive, but I've not seen him for the last two years." She shrugged. "I guess you can say that I don't really have a family who cares for me. Agatha was my nurse," Siena paused, winced, then continued, "Agatha raised me. Even if she isn't related to me by blood, I think of her as my family. She is a good woman."

"I've finished, lass," Fergus said with a broad grin. "Ye held up like a true warrior. Ye can open yer eyes now."

Slowly, Siena turned her head and Roderick smelled the fragrance of flowers wafting from her black hair. She felt right in his arms. He hated to admit it, because it had been a long time since he'd held a woman like this, and something stirred within him. He was momentarily speechless in his surprise.

Then Roderick thought of his dead wife, and the anger he tried so hard to control surged through him like a coiled snake that had been provoked. Fighting his rage, he thought back to that fateful day when he had returned to his holding to find his wife had been raped and murdered and his son missing. Something within him had broken. Gone was any happiness he'd once felt. It was replaced with bitterness and guilt that he'd not been there to protect them.

Roderick shook his head to rid it of the dark images. He'd been bitter for so long that he didn't know how to change. Now he held a woman in his arms, a woman who had killed his mortal enemy. For that, he was grateful, but he felt so strange—something he would sort out later. For now, Siena looked clearly exhausted and pitiful with one swollen eye and a dark circle under the other eye. He shoved to his feet and gently lifted Siena and carried her back to her blanket.

"I will sleep on this side, so we can share my plaid, and my warmth," he said, pointing. "Duncan will sleep next to Agatha. You needna worry about anyone harming ye tonight."

Siena tugged the red plaid over her and tucked it under her chin. Her strength was fading. "It is a great comfort not to worry about our safety. I'm not sure that this is proper, but truth be told, I don't really care tonight," she murmured, her words slurred. "You have been most kind to us, my lord."

Roderick nodded. He probably should have said something more, but he feared what he might say. Though she showed the scars of her beating and misuse by his enemy, he still remembered she was related to the bastard who had killed his wife and compassion was not what he felt at the moment. Instead, he tossed a couple of sturdy logs on the fire so that it would burn all night. Glancing around the campfire he saw his men positioned for sleep, their swords beside them. Fergus would stand watch while they slept.

It was cold tonight. They would be lucky to return home before the first snowfall, Roderick thought as he took his place beside Siena. At least the women were both asleep. Lady Siena needed rest in order to heal. He believed she was too pale, but there wasn't anything he could do about it tonight.

He folded a blanket and placed it under his head. His body was weary, and he thought sleep would be easy, but it didn't come. Instead, his thoughts transported him back to that terrible day more than a year ago.

HE COULD STILL TASTE THE STENCH OF BURNING WOOD AND SEE THE women's bodies in his mind's eye. He had to step over them, searching . . . searching until he found Gillian, her face so swollen he'd barely knew her.

He had blamed himself for not leaving enough men to properly protect his holding that day. Frantically, he had searched for his son. When he couldn't find him, he had found a banner from Fidach, and knew who was responsible. Roderick's men had lost loved ones, as well, and the mood was grim as they began to bury their dead. As dusk fell, Roderick had vowed they would rebuild the holding as it was before.

This time they would paint the walls black so all who saw would remember this terrible day.

His boy, four-year-old Michael had never been found. Roderick had hoped to question Fidach as to what happened to his son before killing the man, but now that opportunity was lost. Somehow, he couldn't bury the past completely. He couldn't see a small child surviving alone, but he still held hope that one day he would find his son alive.

RODERICK SHUT HIS EYES AND PUSHED THE PAST WHERE IT belonged. Then he said a small prayer that his son might be somewhere safe. He glanced at the small woman lying beside him. He had yet to touch her, wondering if there wasn't any part of her that didn't hurt. Her cheek and neck were turning blue, making her a pitiful sight indeed from her beating. She was a Sassenach and his people wouldn't like that fact. What was he to do with her? He didn't know the answer, but he was certain she could make herself useful, and have a better life than she had before.

He gathered that Siena was a healer. Elen, the healer at home, was growing old and in need of help so it could be the perfect place for Lady Siena.

Roderick realized he'd lived for revenge for so long, too long. He sighed. Now it was done, and the man responsible for the attack was dead, he should feel relieved. The relief he expected wasn't forthcoming. He still felt empty inside, and he wondered how it would be to feel something other than anger again.

He rolled over and welcomed the warmth of the small body

beside him. For the first time, in what seemed like forever, he was comfortable enough to sleep. Siena rolled toward him and he wondered if she sought the comfort that another warm body could give her tonight. He draped his arm across her and pulled her next to his side.

Somehow in the midst of all the confusion this felt right, and he felt protective. No one would ever hurt the lass again.

CHAPTER 4

The next morning Roderick woke up to find his arm draped across a warm body snuggled next to him. During the night, Siena had whimpered several times and he had to comfort and assure her that she was safe.

Something changed within him during the night, an overwhelming need to protect Siena seemed natural to him.

It had been too long since he'd known anything but hatred, and he didn't want to disturb this newfound peace, but he knew they couldn't remain here. With his free hand he stroked the side of Siena's face to wake her. She felt much too warm. On second thought, she was downright hot.

He leaned up on his elbow and touched Siena's forehead. Aye, she had a fever. However, there wasn't much he could do until they reached his holding where The Green Woman could attend to her.

Glancing around at the frost-covered campsite, he saw the

first signs of his men waking up to start their day. The fire was no more than embers and ashes.

Carefully, he slid Siena's hand off his chest, then he pushed himself into a sitting position. He reached over and gently shook her. "Wake up, lass. 'Tis morning. We'll be leaving soon."

Siena groaned then slowly opened bloodshot eyes. Her face appeared as pale as the frost and she looked completely drained. However, it would be time to travel as soon as they broke up the campsite, so she must get up and attend to what was necessary before they left. She'd not likely be able to sit a horse for long today without falling off.

Roderick must have awakened Agatha because she sat up and yawned. She stretched her arms overhead, and then she turned toward them, frowning as she recognized how ill her mistress was. "How are you feeling, milady?"

"M--my head hurts. I'm sure it is caused by the fever," Siena said as she glanced toward Agatha. "By chance, did you bring my herbs?"

"There wasn't time for me to fetch anything but our clothes." Agatha shoved herself to her feet, and then ran her hands down her skirt to smooth out the wrinkles. "Let me help you to the stream so you may wash before we leave. The cold water will help you feel better."

"At the moment, I doubt anything will make me feel better," Siena grumbled.

Roderick took Siena's good arm and helped her to her feet. "We have a long ride ahead of us today," he said impatiently. "We should reach my holdin' by nightfall, where my healer can tend to you. Ye are weak, lass, so ye'd best ride with me today."

"Aye." She held her arm up to Roderick, then swayed backward, so he had to steady her. "Do you see any red streaks?"

30

He took her arm gingerly, then partially unwrapped the bandage. *He felt like a servant*, he thought, and questioned the fact that he should be doing such a menial task. Wasn't he called the Devil's Laird? The man who made others tremble by the mere mention of his name. If only they could see him now. For here he stood tending a woman. "Nay," he said as he rewrapped her arm, wondering why he couldn't dismiss her so easily. "Remember, yer body went through a great deal yesterday, and that was before the hanging," Roderick said, shaking his head. "Most would have died."

"I'm made of strong stuff." She half-smiled. "Aye. It was fortunate for me that you showed up when you did."

Roderick made sure Agatha had a good grip on Siena before he turned and left them. There was much to get ready before they rode out.

Siena felt as if she were in a dream world as she stumbled through the trees to the small stream supported by Agatha. Siena also had an odd, sick, empty feeling. Since yesterday her world had come crashing down around her – not that her world had been good before, but she'd had things that were familiar to her. Now she had nothing, only Agatha. She cherished her, but their future was uncertain. They had no home, nothing to hold on to.

Now she was going to an unfamiliar place. What would she find there? Would people mistreat her there as they had in her own home? She didn't have the slightest idea, but she did know she needed some help getting her fever down before she could think straight again. She tore a piece of material off the bottom of her underskirt and bathed herself with cold water. It felt good and reviving, but she was still light-headed, and her eyes burned as though they had sand in them. She wished she could remove her head completely, so it would quit hurting so bad.

"Do you think anyone would notice if I sat down in the middle of the stream?"

"It is much too cold outside, milady. Why would you do such? And where are your shoes?" Agatha asked as she splashed water on her own face. She shivered from the icy drench. "You must get out of the water least you catch your death."

"I'm so hot," Siena complained. "I want to be cool."

"'Tis the fever talking." Agatha took the cloth from Siena and dipped it in the cold water, then she squeezed the water out. "Come milady, you can hold the cool cloth to your head." Agatha gripped Siena firmly by the elbow and slipped the shoes back on her feet. "Let's go to our new home. I'm anxious to see it, and to get warm. I'm not sure I can feel my toes at the moment."

Siena let Agatha steady her as they made their way back to camp. Siena followed Agatha like a small, lost puppy. Then strong arms lifted her off the ground. The next thing she knew she'd been settled in front of Roderick on his giant warhorse. Truth be told, she was glad, so she could rest her head on his chest, but she felt she should protest … just a little. "I should ride my own horse. I don't want to be a bother," she mumbled.

"The black is sturdier than yer palfrey," Roderick explained. "Besides, I'm no sure ye could stay on yer horse for hours without falling off and adding more injuries to what ye already have."

Siena was too tired to protest. Instead, she leaned back and welcomed the strength of his arms supporting her, and strangely enough, she felt safe with someone she'd once thought of as the enemy. The slow steady gait of the horse soon lulled her into a restful sleep.

Roderick really wasn't sure why he didn't let one of the other men carry Siena. They were capable, but for some strange reason he didn't want them touching her. He glanced down at her. She reminded him of a stray animal that someone had thrown out because they didn't want them.

By the end of the day, they would be home where she could receive proper care. In the meantime, she'd better not die on him. He forbade it.

Roderick held his left hand up for the procession to stop. "We'll have to go single file through the pass," he said to Duncan.

Roderick had no sooner gotten the words out of his mouth when Siena jerked to a sitting position, and he had to hold on to her, so she wouldn't fall. The lass was dangerous when she first awoke from sleep.

"You must not go!" she warned him, clutching his plaid.

"Go where, lass?"

"Through the Blue Pass. It is dangerous. They wait to attack you."

"Yer fever has made ye daft," Roderick told her. However, something gave him pause as he looked into her bloodshot eyes. How did she know they were getting ready to go through a pass when she'd been fast asleep?

"Not fever. I saw them."

Roderick was listening now. "Go ahead."

"It's a trap. Five men are waiting to attack you once you proceed through the pass. Be careful," she said the last in a whisper as she collapsed against him.

Duncan had ridden up beside them. "Back at the castle, they said Lady Siena could see things," he said. "Do you suppose…?"

"Ah, wull I'm no' sure I believe in seein' things, but yet --. We'll take no chance. Leave the women here," Roderick said as he turned his mount around. "Gareth, take the men up through the trees and root out what is up there. We'll give ye a head start, and then Duncan and I will ride through the pass. With any luck, that will draw out whoever is there."

Gareth was quick to obey.

They stopped in a small clearing. Duncan spread out two red tartans on the frost-covered ground, and then took the girl from Roderick. Siena moaned. "Och, she still burns with fever."

"Aye, hopefully we will be home before sunset and she can get some rest." Roderick turned. "Agatha, stay here with yer mistress. I'll come back for ye as soon as I know it's safe."

"Don't forget us," Agatha pleaded.

"How could I forget ye?" Roderick said with what he hoped was a smile.

He felt better with his arms free. Now they would see if what Siena had said was true. "I'll go first," Roderick said to Duncan. "Keep an eye out."

The path was wide enough for two, but most of the time they came through the pass single file to be safe. Birch trees were to the left and on the right-side oaks grew out of the sides of the hill. Slowly, they made their way on the winding path. They had barely swung around the bend, when bellowed war cries ripped the air and two men jumped out of the bushes at them.

Roderick nudged Hercules toward the man on the left and lunged off his horse, taking the assailant down. He heard

Duncan cursing and ranting as he swung his sword to end the life of the other man.

Roderick jerked his man up by the front of his shirt. "Who are ye?"

"We heard you have the White Witch."

"I have no witch." Roderick shook the man "Who sent ye?"

The man's eyes were wide with fear, however, he said in a choked voice, "Lord Malcolm needs the White Witch. . . Fidach's sister."

"And the reason he needs her?"

"S--She is the key to finding the Holy Grail."

Roderick straightened, then shoved the man away from him, knocking him on his backside. "Such English nonsense. This day, I will let ye live, and ye can tell Malcolm he need not bother Fidach's sister again. She is under my protection. And she is no witch."

The soldier jumped to his feet, turned, and ran back down the path.

"Let's go back, get the women, and meet up wi' the others," Roderick said. "I dinna think there are any more attackers. The lads did a good job up top."

"Aye. But what about this White Witch?" Duncan asked.

"Sounds like nonsense to me. Remember, we found her ready to be hanged. If there were such things as witches, she'd been able to get away without our help."

"Aye," Duncan said.

It didn't take them any time before they arrived back at the clearing to find the rest of his men and Agatha. "Where is your mistress?" Roderick bellowed, unable to believe that Siena wasn't where he'd left her.

Agatha was ringing her hands, clearly agitated. "T--two

soldiers came and took her, sire. I couldn't stop them." Her lip was bleeding. Evidently, she'd tried to stop them from taking the girl. "They went that way." She pointed.

Roderick blew out his breath in disgust. "The rest of ye take Agatha and head for home. I'm going after my captive."

"Ye need me to ride wi' ye?" Duncan asked.

"Nay. I will make better time by myself. I'll see ye back at Black Dawn."

"The lass is a lot of trouble, and she isn't even conscious." Duncan chuckled. "Canna imagine what it's going to be like once she is alert."

Roderick gave Duncan a half-smile. "Of that, you and I agree. But she is mine, and I dinna appreciate someone takin' her from me."

SIENA AWOKE TO SUFFOCATING HEAT.

She was bundled up much too tight. A flicker of apprehension coursed through her. She needed air. And she needed it now!

"Let me out!" she cried. When she received no response, she began thrashing until her arms were free. How dare Roderick treat her as a sack of grain. Had something happened for him to change his mind? He'd been so gentle when he bandaged her arm this morning . . . now this.

Finally, her head and arms were free of the blanket, and when she could see it wasn't Roderick, she punched the person who held her. "I said to let me out!" She landed a blow to the man's jaw. Her panic had given her strength of two men. The man's head jerked back, and he swore and loosened his grip.

"I cannot hold her," the stranger called out as his horse danced around in a circle. Finally, the animal reared, throwing both of them to the ground.

Siena landed on her back, knocking the breath from her body. It took several gasps before she could breathe again. She didn't recognize these men, so she figured they were some of her brother's thugs. But what disturbed her most was that she had no knowledge of being put on a horse or how she ended up here. She vaguely remembered bathing in a stream this morning, but nothing more.

She realized her fever had broken because her arms were damp from sweat, and her head didn't hurt as it once had. At least she could think clearly now that her mind wasn't in such a haze. However, she had no idea how she was going to get out of this mess.

"W--where is Laird Scott?"

"Dead, we hope," said one of the men.

She swallowed hard. Roderick couldn't be dead, surely these men were lying.

The other man, a dark-skinned soldier said, "Get the White Witch. We need to make time lest our brothers were not successful in killing the Devil's Laird."

"Who are you?" she repeated as she scrambled to her feet and backed away. A wave of apprehension swept through her. She knew she was still weak because she hurt all over but fight them she would. There was no way she would go with these men.

"We were instructed to bring the White Witch to Lord Malcolm," replied the man who had been holding her.

Siena had heard people call her the White Witch before, but she'd never been sure what they meant. However, if these two men thought her a witch, maybe she could use it to her advantage.

Slowly, she straightened and raised her arms over her head. She smiled benignly, as if dealing with temperamental children. She took a deep breath and began to chant in a loud dead voice.

"Whatever evil comes to me.
May it be returned to you three times three."
She pointed at the men.
"To whoever sent you, so mote it be.
That death will come to you and he."

SHE BROKE OUT IN HYSTERICAL LAUGHTER AND TWIRLED AROUND for effect. Her black hair swished straight out as she spun around.

"D--did you hear that James?" the man sputtered. "She is putting a curse on us."

It took two tries before James managed to mount his horse because his foot kept slipping. "Aye. Let's get out of here."

Siena started toward them her hands held out in front of her, repeating her chant. She'd never seen men move so fast as they jerked their horses around and galloped away from her.

That was rather fun.

Siena let her breath out slowly. A little too late, she realized that she should have demanded they leave her a horse. However, she couldn't stay here so she turned and started back the way she'd come, or the way she thought they had come. She wasn't sure what she would find, but the other way would take her back to her home and she definitely didn't want to go back there.

This was the second time in the last few days she'd taken up for herself, and she really liked the feeling of power. A sense of strength came to her and her despair lessened. She swore that from this day forth, she would take care of herself and would never be at the mercy of a man ever again.

Slowly, she put one foot in front of the other, even though they felt very heavy, and headed down the road. She hoped the men were lying about Roderick being dead. She wasn't sure she was worth his effort to save her a second time. Still, she hoped he had Agatha and would be looking for her.

RODERICK COULDN'T REMEMBER WHEN HE'D FELT SUCH AN urgency to find someone other than his family, and that had not turned out well. He would kill the men if they had hurt Siena. He kept reminding himself to be reasonable, but he wasn't listening to himself. Siena was his. And he'd never cared for men taking what belonged to him.

Hercules cantered down the path until Roderick pulled the beast to a halt. He dismounted and checked the ground to see if the tracks were fresh. Rubbing his hand across the dirt, he felt the impressions. There appeared to be two riders, so overcoming them would be simple. *Nothing like a good fight*, he thought as he mounted.

He nudged Hercules with his heels and they were off down the wood covered road. He'd been traveling for a while and growing more irritated by the moment that he'd not caught up with the bandits. Then he spotted someone up ahead.

At last.

Roderick halted ten yards in front of the person. He sensed a trap. However, it appeared to be Siena standing in the middle of the road all by herself with no one around. He reached behind him and pulled out a long dagger and laid it on his leg, so no one could see the weapon.

"Are you alone, Siena?" Roderick shouted.

"Yes."

"Saints above!" he swore to himself. "How had she escaped?" he asked his horse, not expecting a response, but dumbfounded at what he was seeing. She looked like she was taking a stroll down the road. Not very steady, as she was swaying from side to side, but she was on her feet. A great accomplishment, considering he'd last seen her lying on his plaid.

Roderick slipped his knife back in place. He dismounted and walked the short distance over to her. Hercules followed him. He took in her disheveled appearance before he asked, "Are ye hurt?"

"You came for me," she said with a surprised expression. And then she smiled. It was the first time he had seen her do so, and his heart swelled with feelings he'd thought long dead.

"Aye, I came for ye," Roderick replied. "You are my ..." He started to say prisoner, but she wasn't exactly that. "Ah, wull, ye are mine, and I always take care of what belongs to me."

He saw surprise on her face as she said, "Thank you."

There was something odd about this woman. He was glad to see both her eyes were open and clear. He knew the fever had passed. One eye still had a blue-colored bruise, but the swelling had gone down. "Where are the men who took ye?"

"Gone back the way they came."

Something really wasn't making any sense to him. Why

would they go through the trouble of taking her, and then let her go? He would wait and ask her more questions on the ride home. "Here, let me help you in the saddle. I'm glad to see yer fever is gone." He placed his hands on her small waist and lifted her up onto Hercules, and then mounted behind her.

"Yes, but I'm still as weak as a kitten." She sighed. "However, I'm sure I'll feel fine in a few days."

Roderick saw the wild haunted look in her eyes and wondered if she was still afraid. He wrapped his plaid around her and settled her on his lap. Then he turned his mount and they started for home. "Tell me how ye got away, and who or why did they take you?"

When she failed to answer him, he glanced down and saw that again she slept soundly. Evidently, she trusted him to fall asleep so quickly. Since he'd found her, she'd been unconscious or asleep. What would she be like when she was fully awake?

"Perhaps later, I will find out." Roderick chuckled then nudged his horse forward. His questions would have to wait for now.

CHAPTER 5

*S*iena felt herself swaying.

Slowly, she opened her eyes and found she had her arm wrapped around Roderick's back. What must he think of her? Ladies should hold themselves erect and not slouch over a man like she was doing. However, there was something about Roderick that was so warm and comforting that she could stay like this forever. Her heart thumped rapidly as she raised her eyes to his chin.

"I'm so sorry I've dozed off again," she said, feeling Roderick's strength radiating around her. She pulled her arm from around his back. "I realize I have been a lot of trouble." She glanced up at him to see if he was frowning before she rushed on, "I'm surprised you didn't leave me behind."

"I canna deny it has been interestin'," Roderick said with a smile. "A hanging and a kidnapping in two days. Aye, ye do make life fascinating, lass."

"Life hasn't been normal lately, if it ever was."

Siena sat straighter trying to stretch her back the best she could on a horse, bumping Roderick's chin in the process. "Sorry." She felt her cheeks warm with a blush. "Do we have much further to go?"

"Two hours, perhaps." Roderick placed her head back under his chin, and then realized she hadn't answered his question. "Tell me, lass did ye ken those men who kidnapped you?"

"Nay. They kept calling me the White Witch, but as far as I know, I've never seen the men before." She tilted her head to the side like she was trying to figure out something. "How did they take me away from you?"

Roderick decided to ignore her question. "Perhaps, they were friends of yer brother?"

"I have no idea," Siena sighed, then rested her head on his chest, deciding it was much more relaxing than sitting straight up. She couldn't understand why she was so relaxed when she was around Roderick. She'd had very little contentment in her life, but now she would have to admit the coziness of a man's arms around her was very nice.

"How did ye get away?"

"Since they thought I was a witch, I merely acted the part: kind of daft like, waving my hands over my head and chanting a curse." She laughed as she pictured the scene. "You should have seen them run."

Roderick chuckled. "I bet it was a sight." *Strange*, he thought. He'd laughed more in the last two days than he ever had before. It was odd to experience just the slightest bit of mirth when he'd been bitter for so long. He didn't understand how Siena made him feel so different, but she did.

"I did not understand their talk about the Holy Grail," Siena

43

said with a frown. "How would I know anything about a Grail? What where they talking about?"

"The cup of Christ," Roderick said quickly, then when she still looked confused he continued, "'Tis said that he who has the cup will rule the world. The English have searched long and wide for the cup and most have died on their quest."

"And the Scots?"

"Ah wull, we rarely chase after anything other than our enemies."

"And the fairies?"

"Och, ye got me there, lass."

She turned those bright blue eyes up to look at him. "I have no idea why someone would think I could find something that has been lost for hundreds of years."

"Evidently, they think the White Witch can find the Grail."

He saw the worry in her eyes. "We willna worry about it for now. You will be safe with me that I can promise ye."

"You lost me before when those men took me. I'm still not sure how."

Roderick laughed. "'Tis is a long story, lass. If I had been with ye . . . they would never have gotten you."

Siena peered at him doubtfully from beneath her lashes, but she let the subject rest while she settled herself, so she could watch the scenery.

They rode on until a castle loomed ahead. It sat on top of a hill so that it overlooked the valley and the other rolling hills. It looked a lot like an English castle but much larger.

However, Siena couldn't believe what she was seeing. She gasped, "It's black."

"Aye."

"B--But it used to have white walls," Siena said more or less to herself when she realized that she'd been to this very castle before.

"Ye know of Black Dawn, lass?"

"I thought it was called White Dawn."

She felt Roderick tense behind her. He growled, "It was until yer brother attacked my home and burnt most of it to the ground."

"I'm so sorry," she said, but she didn't tell Roderick that she had warned his wife that an attack would happen. Evidently, his wife hadn't mentioned the warning. Now, Siena realized that Roderick was married, and his wife would tell him about her visit as soon as Siena met her. His temper was too bad for her to tell him. Would Roderick blame her too? After all, she had tried to help, but there had been nothing she could do to stop the attack. All she could do was warn his family. Thank God, Roderick didn't question her further.

They rode down the hill and up the next toward the castle. She heard the rattle of chains as the castle gates magically opened without him calling out.

"I guess they knew we were coming," Siena said, thinking how much his home reminded her of an English castle.

"Aye." Roderick nodded. "They can see a great distance from atop the walls, and I have several outposts to watch for visitors approaching the castle."

Roderick said no more as they passed through the lane that lead between the cottages with their thatched roofs which were scattered on both sides of the road and fields in-between some of the huts where crops would be grown in the spring. They continued on over the drawbridge, the horse's hooves sounding sharp on the wooden floor. They rode under the portcullis and into the outer bailey where a large field stood empty.

Siena pointed. "Is that field for crops?".

"Nay, lass. 'Tis where the men practice combat. Most crops are grown by the villagers that we passed, but we do have gardens beyond the keep also.

They climbed a hill that overlooked the training field. Here there were different merchants who stood motionless as they stopped what they were doing to greet their laird while he rode past them. She saw one man with a boot in his hand, which he was putting new leather on the bottom.

Roderick called out to each vassal as they rode past or gave them a friendly nod. He was nothing like his legend of being a devil. He seemed to truly care for his people.

It was her brother who'd been the devil, Siena thought.

They stopped by a long building that appeared to be a stable by the smell. Roderick pulled Hercules to a halt. He lowered Siena to the ground with his left arm. She stood to the side as he dismounted. A short man with a round belly ambled out of the stables with a wooden pitchfork in one hand, which he stabbed into the ground. He wore the Scott's plaid that matched his red hair and beard.

"Ah, welcome home, Laird Scott," he said. "Ye surely huv been missed."

"Garvin, 'tis good to see ye," Roderick replied. He tossed the reins to the man. "Rub Hercules down and give him some extra oats. It has been a long few days." Roderick rubbed the back of his aching neck. He hadn't realized how tired he was until he returned home. It was as if the weight of the world had been sitting on his shoulders and he wasn't sure he knew what normal was anymore. He turned to Siena. "Come, Siena and I'll have a servant find ye a room. I'm sure Agatha is already there waiting for ye."

Siena wasn't certain what to say other than, "Thank you."

Once they entered the great hall, which was twice as big as the one at Berwick, she expected to see his family. However, there was no one to greet them, just the crackling of the fire that looked most inviting to warm their bones.

Roderick nudged her. "Follow me."

Siena smiled to herself. Hadn't she been following him since she had met him? The man sure loved to issue orders.

They climbed stone steps to the second floor, then made their way down a long hall. Roderick stopped in front of an oak door and shoved it open. "I think ye will be comfortable here."

Siena's legs felt like water after climbing the stairs, and it was then that she realized she still wasn't completely well. She sagged against him, longing for the bed. A yellow colored feather comforter was spread over what looked like a very comfortable bed. There was the red Scott plaid that Roderick wore folded across the bottom. She liked that. Had his wife left that feminine touch?

Agatha came bustling into the room, smiling from ear to ear. "I knew he would find you, milady." She opened her arms and gathered Siena into a hug.

"I'm thankful he did."

"I'll have hot water and bandages sent up for yer bath," Roderick said from the doorway. "I will also have Elen look in on ye as she kens the most about healing."

"Thank you." Siena tried to force her confused emotions in order as she sat down on a chair beside the bed. I would like a few days to get my strength back to what it should be," she said, and then added, looking at Roderick. "If you don't mind."

"Aye. I think that is a good idea, lass. You have been through a great deal and rest is probably the best medicine. Food will be sent up so that ye can eat in yer room and rest. We will have plenty of time to talk later," Roderick said, then he turned and shut the door behind him.

———

LATER THAT NIGHT IN THE GREAT HALL, RODERICK AND HIS MEN gathered for dinner. The sounds of men laughing and talking were a good sound to him. He sat behind the high table. There were three long wooden tables in front of his table filled with his men.

They talked among themselves as food was served, and Roderick noticed the tension had eased from his men. Perhaps, they were glad they could put the past behind them now that they had their revenge. He hoped so. He felt a little lighter himself.

Roderick picked up a bannock and spread creamy butter on the bread. He took a bite, savoring the taste of the warm bread, then followed it with a swig of ale.

"Where is yer prisoner?" Duncan asked as he joined his laird.

"She isn't my prisoner."

Duncan took his seat beside Roderick. "Then what is she?"

"You just willna let it go?" Roderick grumbled. "Ye're like a blasted thorn in my side."

"Ah, weel. I like gettin' under yer skin." Duncan grinned, then took a swig of ale.

"If you were not such an old man, I'd knock ye out."

Duncan chuckled. "So, where is the lass?"

"My guest," Roderick said pointedly, "is in her room. I want her fully recovered before she joins us."

"'Tis probably best. Ye have to admit the lass showed strength that she probably wasn't aware of. Not many English-women or men would have survived what she went through."

"I agree. She's a feisty wee lass. Most women would have been in tears."

Duncan tore a bannock apart. "'Tis a shame that we dinna get any information from Fidach."

Roderick stabbed his dirk into a meaty rib and placed it in his trencher before answering. "Aye. Will I ever get any peace over my son?"

Duncan reached over and placed a hand on Roderick's shoulder. "I'm praying one day ye will, son."

A WOODEN BATHTUB HAD BEEN BROUGHT INTO SIENA'S ROOM AND bucket after bucket of hot water was hauled up the stairs and dumped into the tub. Once it had been filled, Agatha helped Siena undress, so she could ease into the hot water.

"Ah, I do believe this water will help with many of my aches," Siena said as she leaned back against the tub and closed her eyes. After a few minutes, Siena said, "Agatha will you wash my hair? I'm trying not to get water on my wound."

"Aye," Agatha said as she reached for a small jar of scented soap. She began to lather Siena's hair. "The warm water must be heaven after the cold loch. Once you have on a clean gown, I know you'll feel much better."

The past few days seemed like a blur. It was as if Siena was reading a book and everything was happening to someone else within the pages. "I think so too. I'm still very tired. I suppose my body needs rest before I'm back to good health. I love the smell of roses from the soap." She wiped the suds from her face. "Have you met the Laird's wife?"

"Nay, milady, I've not seen anyone, other than the servants, since I was shown to this room."

"Have you been free to leave the room?"

"Aye. I don't believe we are prisoners."

By the time Siena had dried off and towel-dried her hair, she was exhausted. She slipped beneath the turned-back covers intending to sleep, however, a sharp knock rattled the door and made her sit back up. She propped upon the pillows behind her, and held her breath, expecting to meet the laird's wife as she bade whoever it was to enter.

The door flew open and a woman dressed in green, with green leaves entwined in her braids, swept into the room and Siena knew right away this wasn't Roderick's wife. This lady was very old, and daft looking with leaves sticking out of her hair here and there. The woman carried a wicker basket full of cream-colored bandages on her arm, so Siena assumed this had to be the healer.

"Good day to ye, Lady Siena. I am Elen." She strolled over to the bed and shooed Agatha out of her way with a wave of her hand. "I'm hundred and three years gone, and my knees are no' what they used to be," Elen said as she sat in the straight-backed chair beside the bed. "Oooch, 'tis better. Our laird asked that I look in tae see if I can help with yer wound. He seemed most concerned."

"I think I'm fine. Or will be." Siena added. "I have a gash on my arm." She held her arm up, feeling much like a child. "I am a healer, myself, but of course, it's hard to stitch my own arm. Fergus was kind enough to do the sewing and I think he did a good job, but I'm without my herbs and I worry about infection." She realized she was rambling, so she stopped talking.

"Laird Roderick did mention yer wound and also a fever. Do ye mind if I have a look?"

"Please do."

Elen first felt Siena's forehead. "I feel no fever, so that is good, lass." Elen carefully removed the bandages and examined the red and tender injury.

"Milady," Agatha said from the doorway. "I'm going to take a walk outside while you have someone with you. I think the night air will do me some good." Siena nodded, and Agatha left the room.

Siena watched as Elen worked. There was something comforting about the old woman's touch. Her hands were weathered, and her hair snow-white, but her smile was kind and understanding. Siena glanced at Elen's long braids wrapped upon her head where the leaves were entwined.

"Why do you have leaves in your hair?" Siena asked and then caught herself. "I'm so sorry. That was terribly rude."

Elen glanced up. She had the kindest eyes that were as green as moss on a sunny day. Her eyes were sharp in her lined face not dulled by age.

"Always ask questions, lass. 'Tis the only way tae learn," Elen said as she reached into her basket and pulled out a small jar. "I'll answer yer questions in a moment, but first let me say that your wound shows no infection. I'm going to put some *Dubhan ceann-cósach, Dubhan Pecan-dubh* over the stitching."

"I'm afraid you'll have to explain. I have no idea what you just said," Siena said with a laugh.

"Ye, dinna speak Gaelic, lass." Elen chuckled. "Weel, 'tis an all-heal salve I mixed up using an herb called *Prunella vulgaris* and some goldenrod. I make this paste for cuts and large wounds." She opened the jar and showed it to Siena. "Works nicely." She carefully spread the yellow-tinged salve on Siena's arm, then reached in her basket and pulled out several cloth bandages.

"I have used goldenrod before," Siena said as she watched the woman wrap her arm. "I'm afraid that in our haste we didn't have time to get my herbs. I will have to gather some of my own herbs if I'm to be of any help around here." She examined her arm. "I must say the salve is soothing and cool."

"I'll huv to show ye where ye can find the best herbs come spring. I'm glad Laird Roderick has brought home someone useful. Still, with ye being a Sassenach, folks willna be trusting of ye."

"I know," Siena said with a shrug, "but maybe with time, I'll be accepted."

"What are those marks on yer throat, lass? I think my cream could help them also."

Siena knew her face must have turned beet red because she could feel the heat burning her cheeks. "Well, my brother's men were trying to have me hanged when Laird Roderick came to my rescue."

Elen's white eyebrows shot up. "That's quite a tale, lass. Why don't ye start from the beginning and tell me what happened to ye, that is, if ye dinna mind. I've never heard of such a thing."

Normally, Siena would not talk about herself, but there was something about the healer that made her comfortable. Slowly, Siena told the old woman about her life. Elen patiently listened and nodded here and there, but she never showed any shock. Siena thought she would see judgment in Elen's eyes, but Siena was wrong.

"Ah, lass," Elen said shaking her head. "Ye've been through a great deal. Yer brother was not liked by my kind. 'Tis glad I am that he is dead." She held out her hand. "Let me see this mark that ye referred to."

Siena twisted her left arm and held it up to Elen. "They call it the mark of the devil."

"That isn't what it is." Elen extracted a pipe out of her pocket. She paused a moment to pick up a straw which she held to the candle's flame on the bed stand. She lit her pipe and puffed a couple of times until she blew out a thick, white smoke ring. "The pipe helps me relax. Tonight, I have mint and lavender in the pipe. 'Tis nice. Remember I'm one hundred and three, so relaxing is a must for my weary bones." She nodded toward her pipe. "Now where were we ... Oh, I remember this mark means you are gifted and that ye're a seer? 'Tis an arrow and not a pitchfork, as ye've been led to believe. I've seen it twice before. Huv ye never seen things that are not happening around you?"

"Aye." Siena nodded. "But I never know when I'm going to see things or how it works. It just happens. I have no control over it."

"Ye can practice. In time, ye'll huv much better control." Elen patted her hand. "Ye might not have had a good life in the past, but I believe that it will be better in the future."

"Anything would have to be better than what I left." Then Siena thought of something else. "They also call me the White Witch."

"Alas, people love to put labels on things they dinna understand. "They call me The Green Woman, hence the leaves in my hair, amber around my neck and I dress in green." Elen smiled. She clamped the pipe between her teeth, then pulled the covers back over Siena. Reaching into the basket, Elen brought out a small cup full of liquid and handed it to her. "It's cold and would be better if it were warm, but drink this."

"What is it?"

"Heather tea. It will help give ye restful sleep."

Siena took several sips and then handed the cup back. "It doesn't taste so bad."

"Aye. 'Tis white heather, and scarce. But 'tis magical," she lowered her voice as if telling a secret. "It only grows on the grave of a fairy."

Siena could only stare at Elen, having no idea whether to believe her or not. Things were strange in this land. For all she knew it could be true.

"Why don't ye slide under the covers and sleep. 'Tis still the best cure for many of your aches and pains." Elen stood, then she grabbed the back of the chair to steady herself. Damn knees," she swore. "I'll look in on ye again in the morning."

Siena fell asleep before the door closed.

CHAPTER 6

For three days, Siena slept, waking only to eat and when Agatha would nudge her to make certain Siena was still alive. She would wake up screaming, caught in one of her hellish nightmares, but Agatha was always there to soothe her and remind Siena they were no longer under her brother's command. Sleep became her friend while her body and mind healed.

However, on the fourth day, Siena awoke feeling much better. Slowly, she sat up, stretched, and then looked around the room. Nothing looked familiar to her, and for a second she panicked until she remembered she was at Black Dawn and not Berwick Castle. She looked toward heaven and thanked God for that small blessing.

As Siena tried to move, she had to admit that she felt a little stiff, and sore. Her stomach grumbled. Now she wanted food instead of dreading the idea of eating. Another sign she was feeling like herself once again.

Siena slipped out of bed, paused for a moment until her head stopped spinning, then she padded across the floor to the dry sink. Glancing around for a pitcher, she spotted it on the hearth; thankfully the servants had built a long-lasting fire and had placed the pitcher of water on the hearth to warm. The fire made the room cozy.

She picked up the white pitcher and returned to the basin where she poured water into the large bowl. The wind whistled outside. The sound made her shiver, and she was glad for the warm water. However, her feet were already getting chilled from the cold stone floor, so she knew it must be really cold outside.

Sienna splashed water on her face to wash away the last vestiges of sleep. She reached for her hairbrush, and began brushing her hair, trying to remove the many tangles that had formed from her tossing and turning in bed. She wondered where Agatha was this morning.

As if she'd conjured her up, Agatha dashed into the room. "Praise the Lord, you're awake." She leaned against the wall holding her chest. "When I heard a noise, I thought you had fallen out of bed."

Siena watched Agatha in the mirror before turning on the stool to look at her. "I'm sorry, I've put you through so much worry, but you can stop worrying because I'm feeling much better today." Siena turned back and placed the hairbrush back on the tabletop. "Did Elen come back to see me?"

"Aye, she did. She declared you were doing well." Agatha chuckled. "You slept all the way through her prodding, causing us to wonder how long you were going to sleep. However, Elen said it was good for your body to rest, so she didn't wake you."

"I don't remember a thing."

"Laird Scott will be pleased to hear you're out of bed."

"Really?"

"Aye, he has come by every day to see how you're doing," Agatha said. She went to another room, then returned with a trencher. "Here is some food for you, milady. You must be hungry. I've not been able to get you to eat anything but a few sips of broth."

Siena gratefully ate breakfast consisting of bannocks, butter, and blackberry jam. It was the first time that she'd had a bannock. It reminded her of a scone with a nutty flavor. After the first bite, she sighed. She couldn't remember when food had tasted so good. She licked the butter from her fingers, then drank a glass of goat's milk before saying to Agatha, "I would like to go outside for some fresh air after we dress. I'm not sure how far I can walk, but I need to get my strength back somehow."

"I'm sure that would be wonderful." Agatha stood. "I've not been outside much myself. I'll go and fetch our cloaks and gloves for it's very cold outside this morning."

SIENA GRABBED HER DARK PURPLE CLOAK LINED WITH SILVER FOX and slipped it on. It was the warmest thing she'd ever had and her nicest garment. She had been told that it belonged to her mother making it a cherished belonging.

They stepped through the castle's doorway into a bright winter's day. Siena shivered as the first blast of cold air hit her face. She squeezed her eyelids tight against the bright sunshine. When she finally opened her eyes again, she could see much better after she dashed the tears away from her eyes. Evidently, she'd been in a warm room too long, and that made the wind seem so much colder, but this morning she didn't care. It felt glorious to be alive. "Isn't it wonderful to be outside in the fresh air?"

"Aye, you were never one to stay inside for long periods," Agatha said, pulling her hood over her head.

"It was easier to escape my brother when I was outside." Siena laughed, realizing for the first time that she was free of his torture. Maybe that was why she felt so happy today. She no longer had that sick feeling in the pit of her stomach. It felt good to be alive.

A commotion sounded behind them, causing Siena to turn. There was an ox-drawn wagon loaded with barrels coming to a stop outside the great hall. Siena nodded to the driver but didn't receive any acknowledgement in return. She wasn't sure what she expected since no one here knew her.

"I believe the Scotts like their drink, if that wagon is any indication," Agatha said.

Siena nodded. "I think you're correct. Let's walk a while before we have to go back inside. I must stretch my legs to get the blood flowing again. I feel as if I've been inside for weeks."

They stopped at the stables where Siena went inside to visit her horse and found Hercules was there as well. She rubbed Hercules's soft muzzle. The man she'd seen when they first arrived approached her. He wore a brown jacket and the red plaid that the Scotts wore. His cap was also a red plaid.

"I see he likes ye, lass. Ye must be good wi' horses, cause Hercules dinna let anyone touch him." He shook his head. "Nope, no one at all except me and the laird. His name suits him as he is a devil of stallion."

"I do love horses," Siena said, rubbing the horse's muzzle. "I don't believe we were introduced the other day. My name is Lady Siena." She didn't bother with a last name not wanting to make enemies before people got to know her.

"My name is Garvin. I be the head groomsman, milady." He bowed his head curtly, and added, "I'll take good care of yer horse. Ye needn't fear. I think she's taken a fancy to Hercules. After ye arrived, I put her in a stall at the end and she pitched a right good fit." Garvin paused, then chuckled. "So, I let her out. And you know what she did? She sauntered down to Hercules' stall and stood there." He nodded at the horse. "Guess the lass was tellin' me what she wanted, so I put her in the stall next to him and she settled right down."

Star stuck her head out upon hearing her mistress' voice. Siena moved over to the other stall. Star nudged Siena. "I'm sorry, she has caused you so much trouble," Siena said, kissing the animal. "She is a bit feisty."

"What do ye call her, milady?"

"Her name is Star."

"Aye, it fits her wi' her silver coat. She's a rare one," Garvin held his palm out, so the horse could have a carrot. "Not sure I've ever seen another horse like her. Most are white but she's silver."

"I thought so, too." Siena gave Star a final pat. "Thank you for your time, Garvin. We won't trouble you any longer." Siena smiled at Garvin and asked, "Do you know where your laird has gone?"

"Aye, he is training wi' his men in the outer bailey, milady." Garvin pointed to his left. "Just follow the road to the end and ye'll be on a hill that overlooks the training field. Ye can't miss it."

"Are you feeling all right, milady?" Agatha asked when they turned to leave. "You look a little pale."

"I'm fine," Siena sighed, but admitted to herself that she was very tired. However, she wasn't ready to return to the keep. "That rest at the stable helped."

They passed the blacksmith who was hammering on a horseshoe. They heard the sizzle as he shoved a finished horseshoe into water to cool. Next was the master shoemaker where the smell of leather was strong. There were several other stalls, everyone busy with their daily chores, but they took time to glance at the ladies. Finally, they reached the outer bailey where cottages were scattered about.

"Have ye noticed how everybody has turned to stare at us?"

Agatha nodded. "Aye, but I do not know if it is because we're strangers or maybe they know who we are. I'm sure Fidach wasn't well liked here."

Siena sighed. "Aye. I don't want to have to go through that again. I want to feel as though we belong someplace."

Making their way through the little village, they climbed to the top of a hill, overlooking the brown field down below where men were training. They were throwing spears and fighting with swords; the clanging of metal upon metal sounded loud, even at their distance. It wasn't long before Siena spotted Roderick among his men. He was the tallest, of course, and there was something about him that made you know that he was the commander. She liked his long, brown hair and the way it curled just under his ears. The bright sun brought out the red highlights in his hair as he moved through his drills. When he turned, she saw his firm jaw and the way he carried himself. Aye, he was the commander. Siena smiled. She couldn't wait to talk with him again, and that was something she had never thought about any man before. She usually kept her distance where men were concerned, thinking most might be like her brother.

"No wonder they don't get hurt, milady," Agatha commented. "They fight as if it's a true battle and they don't seem to notice it's cold outside."

"I'm sure the swords are not sharp. They wouldn't want to lose men in a mock battle when there is enough bloodshed in real ones. Look over there." Siena pointed. "They are practicing with bows and arrows."

"I see that," Agatha said. "But I'm sure you could still best them, milady. I've never seen anyone better than you with a bow."

As if he sensed someone watching him, Roderick turned and looked her way, but instead of waving, he grabbed an arrow, placed it on the bow that he'd snatched from one of his men and pulled back the string. In the blink of an eye, he'd aimed at her and let the arrow go.

What! Her mind screamed, and then everything happened in slow motion.

"Get down, milady!" Agatha yelled, shoving the shocked Siena to the ground.

Siena cried out in fright. She couldn't move from the shock. There was a bellow from below, much like a war cry, and a scream behind her. Why would Roderick try to kill her when he'd just saved her life? Something didn't make a bit of sense.

Thank goodness, Siena's wits returned quickly. She heard screaming from behind her, and this time the scream wasn't hers.

She didn't have a chance to get to her feet because Roderick and Derrick were already beside her. Roderick pulled her to her feet and then steadied her, so she wouldn't fall back down. "Are ye all right, lass?"

Siena pulled back and glared at him, expecting to see anger in his eyes not concern. "I—I think so." Her chin jutted out. "Why did you shoot at me?"

Roderick chuckled.

Siena scowled. How dare he laugh at her. She didn't think her question was funny at all. The bloody man had shot an arrow at her head, and if not for Agatha, he could have killed her. "I don't see the humor in you trying to kill me," she snapped.

"I've gone to too much trouble to kill ye, lass." He turned her around. There lying on the ground behind them was a woman with an arrow protruding from her arm. "She was getting ready to stab ye in the back." He pointed to the knife lying in the dirt beside her.

"Milord, I'm so sorry," the woman whimpered. "Please don't punish me."

Roderick set Siena aside and stepped over to the woman on the ground. "Helen, ye dare to attack someone under my protection? Ye should be glad I dinna kill ye."

"Ooo," Helen moaned. "But she is Fidach's sister. Her brother murdered my son. And ye promised all of us revenge, yet ye bring her here to the castle."

"Aye, I did promise ye. However, once I arrived at her brother's castle, Lady Siena had already killed her own brother. By doing so, she destroyed our enemy. Ye should be thanking her not trying to kill her." Roderick turned to Derrick. "Take Helen up to the keep," he ordered with a wave of his hand, "so someone can mend her arm."

"I can mend her arm," Siena said.

Roderick whipped around. "Ye would mend Helen's arm after she attacked you?"

"I'm sure Helen is sorry now that she knows I have no love for my brother." Siena glanced down at the woman on the ground and said, "I would probably have felt the same."

Duncan snapped the arrow shaft and pulled it from Helen's arm. After he tied a cloth around her wound, he tossed the woman over his shoulder and headed back toward the castle. Helen continued to cry out, "I'm sorry, milord. Truly."

"I will go and get your things ready," Agatha said as she hurried to catch up with Duncan.

"Come and walk with me back to the great hall," Roderick said, taking Siena's elbow. "I want everyone to see that you're with me, so we dinna have to worry about yer safety again. From now on, one of my men will be with you when you go outside."

"I'm sorry. I do not want to be trouble."

"Lass, it's been an adventure since I first laid eyes on ye."

"I can't promise that will change, but I'm a good healer, and I would like to take care of your people. With your permission, that is."

"Aye. I think that is a grand idea." He nodded. "Elen has complained for years that she needs help. I'm sure she's told you she's 105." He smiled, and Siena found him so handsome and devilish all at the same time. He took her breath away.

"Actually, she told me she's 103."

Roderick chuckled. "Proves my point that her memory is slipping with the passing years."

Once they had reached the castle's steps, he stopped. 'Tis good to see ye up, lass. I will leave ye here wi' yer patient and return to my men." He looked at her for a moment as if he were trying to figure something out, then added. "I look forward to yer company tonight at dinner."

Siena nodded because she couldn't think of anything to say. Roderick made her feel things she'd never felt before. His smoldering black eyes seemed to capture hers, her heart turned over in response. Every time he talked to her all her sad thoughts floated away. She shouldn't have these feelings when he was married, and most likely, she would be meeting his wife tonight.

That thought made her sad.

CHAPTER 7

Siena dressed in a cream-colored gown with a light blue bliaut. She wore a braided belt of the same material draped on her hips. It felt good to be dressed in something other than the drab gray she'd worn today.

"Please do something special with my hair," Siena said.

"I take it you want to look your best tonight, milady?"

"Yes. I'm not sure why, but I feel nervous as if I'm seeing everyone for the first time."

Agatha laughed. "How about the first time you have actually been awake?"

Siena smiled. "Well, that is true." She wasn't sure why it was so important for her to look her best, but she did want to make a good impression on Roderick's family. So far, he'd been kind to her, however, she wasn't a relative; therefore she wasn't sure what that meant for her future.

After getting final approval from Agatha, the two of them made their way downstairs. Once they were on the steps leading to the great hall, they stopped and looked at all the long tables that were already filled with brawny soldiers. Black Dawn's great hall was so much larger than the one back home. She supposed Roderick did have more men to feed. There were four long, wooden tables plus the high table.

The high table stood upon a wooden platform to one side of a massive stone fireplace, which was ablaze with a roaring fire. Roderick was seated at the table with his back to a stone wall. The candles held in loops on the wall brackets bathed the room in light along with the tripod candlesticks on the tables.

Roderick glanced up and motioned for her and Agatha to join him. Carefully, they made their way among the tables, listening to the grumbles as some of the bigger men had to lean in, so she could pass by them. She noticed that the rushes were clean and smelled of fresh mint, which was very nice and much different from home. Her brother's men had been pigs when it came to eating. She'd usually eaten in her room to avoid them.

"Where shall I sit, milord?"

"Why don't you and Agatha sit here. He pointed to the chairs on his right."

"But, sire," Agatha protested. "Should I sit at the high table?"

"If I commanded it," Roderick replied. "We are not that formal here. Ye are my guest, so please have a seat."

Siena noticed the chair to his left was also empty. Tonight, she would meet his wife. She couldn't remember the woman's name, but she did remember that she had been very pretty, and lucky to have someone strong like Roderick to protect her.

"'Tis good to finally have ye dining with us," Roderick said. "How are ye feelin'? You are not as pale as ye were this afternoon." He couldn't believe how beautiful Siena appeared tonight. There was still a little discoloring under one of her eyes, but other than that she had healed nicely. Where her hair had been dull before, now it was a glossy color that was as black as a raven's wing, and when she turned his way, he noticed her eyes appeared silver as if they glowed.

"I'm much better, thank you," she said. "I'd probably be dead if not for you."

It took Roderick a few minutes before he remembered he'd asked her a question. The woman made his mind meander and that was never a good thing for a warrior. Warriors should not feel anything, and to let their minds wander could get them killed. He would have to work on that problem and remember his discipline. But Siena's eyes seemed to capture him as they changed from silver to clear blue.

"Did yer patient give ye any more trouble?" he asked, breaking the spell.

"Nay." She shook her head. "Helen was as docile as a kitten; however, I was wise enough not to turn my back on her until I was sure she didn't want to kill me anymore."

He nodded his approval. "'Twas probably a wise thing. My clan has hated yer brother for a long time."

Siena saw Duncan approaching the table. She smiled. There was something about Duncan that she really liked. Perhaps, he reminded her of the kind of father she wished she'd had, and she found it comforting to have him near.

"I see we have lovely ladies with us tonight," Duncan said. "'Tis better than seeing all these grumpy old faces all the time." He motioned toward the tables in front of him. "'Twill make the food twice as good tonight, I'd wager," he finished as he sat down next to Agatha.

"You have a sly tongue." Agatha laughed, as did Roderick.

"Ye have the measure of him, Agatha," Roderick leaned

forward so he could see Duncan. "How did the lads do wi' training?"

"They still prefer the swords and spears." He shrugged and added, "The bows and arrows are no to their liking."

"Siena is excellent with a bow and arrow," Agatha boasted.

Roderick looked down at Siena. "Is that so?"

Siena felt her cheeks burn. "Aye."

"Then ye'll have to show me one day."

A horn blew to signal the time for 'washing hands' immediately followed by the servants with ewers, basins, and towels for everyone to wash their hands. Next, trenchers were passed out. They were made from large loaves of stale bread with the middle taken out so there would be someplace to hold the food. Then came the platters of meat that were set in several places down the long table, followed by plates of cheese and vegetables. Then their cups were filled with ale.

Siena pulled her knife from her belt and began to sample the food. She had eaten some of the mutton and found everything very tasty. The fact that Roderick's family had not joined them still bothered her. Siena felt as though she was sitting on pins and needles waiting to meet his wife again. When she could stand it no longer, she asked in a soft voice so only Roderick could hear, "Is your wife not joining us?"

Roderick froze. She could see a muscle twitching in his jaw as he turned to her, and the fury she saw in his eyes frightened her. She leaned back afraid he might strike her. "D--did I say something wrong?"

"I have no family."

"But—"

"Do ye no remember me telling you that yer brother attacked my castle?"

"Aye, but--"

"And yet ye dare to ask about my family! How do ye ken my wife?"

"I—"

Roderick stood, then reached down and grabbed Siena's arm. "Come with me."

Siena didn't have much of a choice as she followed Roderick. She knew everyone in the hall was watching them. They marched straight up the stairs to one of the solars before Roderick turned on her and said, "How do ye know Gillian?"

Siena rubbed her arm where he'd grabbed her. "I will tell you what you want to know when you quit shouting. I assure you there is nothing wrong with my hearing."

"I'm no shoutin'!" Roderick shouted.

Siena crossed her arms and waited and without thinking said, "My brother always shouted at me, too. You saw what happened to him."

Roderick blew out his breath and waited until he'd calmed down. He should hate this woman, but he didn't. However, it was difficult to hold his temper when his wife was mentioned. He took a deep breath and said, "Go ahead."

"I had heard my brother talk about attacking White Dawn a week before he did so. I had a dream about your family, so I went to find them." She held up her hand when Roderick started to speak. "Do not ask me how I made the distance on my own. It is one of those things I cannot explain ... just like when I saw your attack . . I can't explain some of the things I do or see. But, somehow, I made it to your castle. I spoke with your wife and I told her of the coming attack. I thought, perhaps, she could hide and warn the others."

"She knew?" Roderick whispered, feeling he'd been slammed in the gut. His wife knew and yet she died.

"Aye. I told her, and she asked me to take your son to the small cave and hide him. She said she would follow as soon as she warned everyone. That is why I haven't understood why I've not seen your family."

"My wife was raped and killed by *yer* brother," he bit out. "It wasna a pretty sight."

Siena gasped. Her hands flew to her mouth. "Why didn't she run and hide?"

"I dinna ken." Roderick shut his eyes for a moment, seeing the horrors of that day. He shook his head, feeling dead inside. "My son, Michael."

Tears sprung to Siena's eyes. "Did he survive?"

"We've never found him or his body."

Siena dashed the tears from her eyes. "I--I took him to the cave as your wife requested. I wrapped him up and gave him his stuffed bunny. I told him his mother would be along shortly and stressed he should be quiet because it was dangerous. He nodded that he understood and hugged his toy close."

"We searched everywhere, but found nothing," Roderick said. "Can ye show me the cave? I think I ken the one, but I want to make sure."

"I can show you." Siena dabbed at her tears, then her head jerked up. "But if you found no body then Michael could still be alive."

Roderick rubbed the back of his neck. Would he ever find peace? "I dinna see how he could have survived."

"I wish I could tell you what happened, but it's been over a year. I went back home not wanting to be caught by my brother's men. Perhaps I should have stayed . . . I'm sorry."

They both grew quiet.

"It was all my fault," Roderick admitted in a dull and troubled voice.

"How so?"

"I was arrogant enough to believe that my castle would never fall. I dinna leave enough men to protect it. That will never happen again. I've worked hard to double my army since that time."

She placed her hand on his arm. "You cannot blame yourself for my evil brother's doings. Now I wish my vision had been about you, then I could have warned you."

Siena's heart went out to Roderick. For once he'd let his guard down, and she could see the hurt he was experiencing. She wanted to wrap her arms around him to give comfort, but she knew for now he fed off his loss and that is what drove him. She let her arm drop back to her side.

"Perhaps if I really concentrate, I can see what happened to Michael. Maybe he was taken. I would have seen him if he'd been brought to Berwick, so I know he isn't there. I'll need Elen's help, but I promise I will try."

"I'll hope for the best, lass. Ye are dismissed for now," Roderick said, turning his back on her, wanting to be alone.

CHAPTER 8

*S*iena moaned as she rolled over and opened her eyes to the shadows of light peeking out from the window where a shutter had come loose. She hadn't slept well at all last night. The reason was simple, she couldn't get Roderick off her mind. One minute he was angry with her and the next he was holding her telling her everything would be all right. She lay in the drowsy warmth of her bed, thinking. Should she have stayed with the child until his mother came? That was something she would never know, but for now a stab of guilt still lingered deep inside her. Instead of saving them as she had intended . . . in the end the warning hadn't done any good.

Agatha entered the room. "Good morning. It's freezing in here." She went to the window and closed the shutter.

Siena threw back the covers and slid out of bed, then grumbled, "Burr, it is cold." She stumbled over to the fireplace and stirred the embers to get the flames going, then tossed more wood on the fire.

"What happened last night after you left the table with Laird Scott?" Agatha asked. She held a robe up so Siena could slip it on. "He looked very angry."

"He was angry." Siena tied the sash of the robe. "He told me that Fidach killed his wife, and he doesn't know what happened to his son." She sighed. "He said they never found the child's body."

"Oh, no." Agatha visibly blanched. "I'm so sorry, milady." Her face changed from sad to full of contempt as she continued, "We both know your brother was capable of killing the child."

"If only I could picture the boy and see what happened to him." Siena paused to splash water on her face, then patted it dry. "At least, I could bring Roderick a little comfort. I feel so guilty that I didn't do more than I did. Somehow this seems all my fault."

Agatha placed a hand on Siena's arm. "You thought you were doing the correct thing by warning them cf the attack. You couldn't have known that they wouldn't take your warning. And if Fidach had caught you, he would have killed you. I've no doubt of that."

"I know, but I still feel bad." The child's name lingered around the edges of her mind. "Help me get dressed," Siena said, then added, "I'm going to see Elen." Siena had made up her mind that she needed some help. "Do you know which room belongs to Elen?"

"Aye, milady," Agatha said as she slipped a pale yellow bliaut over Siena's head. "This wool will feel good, today. It is very cold this morn."

"Thank you, but you didn't answer my question."

Agatha ran her hands down the bliaut to smooth it out.

"Elen lives in the treatment room, milady. Remember where you treated that nasty woman who tried to kill you?"

Siena smiled at Agatha's indignation. "How could I forget that?"

SIENA MADE HER WAY DOWN A SECOND SET OF STAIRS, WINDING through the hallways until she found Elen's room. When she'd been down here before, the door had been open, but this time it was closed, so she knocked and waited until she heard someone call out to enter.

Slowly, Siena slipped into the room. The many shelves along the walls were filled with different size jars lining the shelves, which she assumed contained lots of herbs for healing. There were two beds in the middle of the room for the sick that were neatly made and thank goodness empty.

"Milady," Elen called from the corner of the room. She'd been sitting on a third bed shoved against an outer wall. "I was wonderin' when I'd see ye again."

"Good morning," Siena said. "I didn't see you when I first entered."

"I've not lit all the candles yet, lass. I should request a room with a window." Elen smiled. "At least I'd have more light down here."

"I agree, nothing like fresh air to help the sick. Why are you way down here?"

"'Tis the safest place in the castle and when yer the only healer they tend to make sure no harm can come to ye."

Elen withdrew a clay pipe and lit the herbal blend with a straw.

"Do I smell mint?" Siena sked.

"Aye, 'tis a special blend along with Horehound and mullein, passionflower and a few other things that help me breathe." After she took several puffs, she asked, "Now, what can I help ye with, lass?" She waved her hand toward a chair. "Please sit down."

Siena chose one of the green cushioned chairs. As a matter of fact, now that she glanced around the room, there was a lot of green. "I didn't notice when I was in here before, but everything is green."

Elen chuckled. She sat on a chair across from Siena. "Remember, I'm called The Green Woman and for that reason ye see green everywhere ye look, but I dinna have antlers growing out of my head as is rumored."

"Thank goodness." Siena laughed.

"The green makes one feel better. Do you see how ye have relaxed since ye entered my room?"

Siena nodded.

"How can I help ye?"

"Everyone tells me that I have special powers. However, I don't know how to use them...."

"I sense there is more?"

"Aye, Roderick told me about his wife and son last night," Siena paused, glancing down at her hands. "I had no idea of his wife's death, and he said he never found his son."

"'Tis sad. Laird Scott worshiped both his wife and son, Michael; however, the laird canna put the past behind him wi' his son still missin'. And I sense he's finally ready to move forward."

"That is why I've come to you." Siena peered into Elen's

green eyes. "I thought perhaps you could show me how to find out what happened to his son."

"Umm," Elen murmured. She took a drag from her pipe, then she blew a smoke circle, which slowly rose until it surrounded her head. "As ye know lass, I'm not a seer, I'm a healer, but ye, lass have been blessed wit' both powers. 'Tis rare." She paused to blow another smoke ring. "'Twould help if ye had seen the wee one."

"But I have." Siena told Elen all about what had happened when she visited Black Dawn before.

Elen sat a little straighter. "Did ye enter by the kitchen or the front door?"

"By the kitchen. I remember the cook went and got her mistress. Why do you ask?"

"'Tis considered unlucky to enter the house by the back door when ye come the first time, which is why ye see so many come through our front doors."

"I didn't know that," Siena said, but wondering why in the world that would matter to anyone. Perhaps it was Elen rambling. "But my warning did no good. However, you survived. What did you do that day?"

"Gillian did warn me, but I chose to remain below, knowing they would not bother to look down here, and I was correct. They did not. She said she was going to warn a few others and then head to the caves for Michael." Elen sighed. "I guess she tarried too long and before she knew it the invaders were upon her."

"It is very sad."

"I think ye need a fairy stone."

Siena looked at her puzzled. "I don't understand."

"We're lucky to have a fairy mound, although, most cannot

see the fairies, I can." Elen smiled. "And I bet ye can, too. Let me fetch my tartan and we will go and see them."

"I've never believed in fairies."

"Ye will, lass. Wait and see."

They left out of the kitchen door and strolled across a courtyard that was used for a garden. In the middle of the stone wall stood an iron gate that was ajar. They pushed it open with a screechy protest and slipped through the gate. A big wall surrounded the entire castle, so they headed toward the wall. Once they got closer, Siena spotted a mound that should have been brown since it was winter, but it was as green as a summer day.

"'Tis said that the fairies were once proud angels who wanted their own kingdom. The fairies that live here are called '*Gude Wichts*,' Elen explained before she called out, "Barra."

Suddenly, six fairies flew up out of the earth, all dressed in green. They were maybe six inches high with big wings that fluttered constantly.

Siena was stunned but recovered quickly as she watched the creatures bob up and down until a girl with long, golden hair moved to the front.

"Elen. How nice to see you?" Barra turned. "I see you have brought a guest who can see us; therefore, she must be special."

"Aye. This is Lady Siena and I believe she has the power to be a healer and a seer, however, she has trouble controlling her powers," Elen explained, then she turned to Siena.

"This is Barra," Elen said with a swish of her hand.

"Hello, Barra," Siena said.

"Milady, you seek my help?"

"If you can help me ... I'd be most grateful."

"Will you permit me to land on your hand, Siena?" Barra asked.

Siena nodded and held out her arm. Barra flew over and landed on the back of Siena's hand. It tickled, but Siena kept her hand steady as not to make the fairy frightened.

"Ah, I sense great strength in you, milady, and you will do good things. Therefore, you will always have our help when you need us."

"Thank you."

Barra withdrew a pink stone, a yellow-colored stone, a blue stone, and a red ruby stone and placed them on Siena's palm, then she flew back to the others. "Always keep the stones with you and turn them over and over in your hand when you need something. There is magic inside the stones. Just as there is magic inside yourself but tell no one that you have them."

Siena examined the pink stone. It was very pretty and smooth. It looked like there were sparkles on the inside trying to escape. "Thank you. I hope one day that I become the person that everyone thinks I am."

"Give it time," Barra said, then she looked at Elen. "I believe it is getting ready to snow, Elen. Best get back to the castle. You know how your bones ache in the cold." Then in a swoosh the fairies had all disappeared, however giggles could be heard beneath the mound.

ONCE THEY WERE SAFELY BACK IN THE CASTLE, ELEN SAID, "SUCH a powerful gift ye have." She wrinkled her nose and nodded as if she came to a conclusion. "I think ye should go back to the cave and find the verra spot where ye left Michael. Look around for something the child might have touched like a smooth stone. Take the stone and keep turning it over and over in yer hand. If you still have no visions, then bring the stone back with ye and we'll try a couple of other things. Perhaps the fairy's stones will help. However, it might take time to learn the way of the stones."

Siena stopped in front of Elen's room. "Thank you for helping me. Roderick wanted to go to the cave so perhaps we can go today. Let's hope I can learn something that will be useful."

"I sense a storm is brewin' like the fairies thought, so do be careful," Elen said. Aye, she thought there was a storm brewing both outside and with the laird.

She smiled. 'Twas time someone stirred her laird in wanting to live again.

SEVERAL HOURS HAD PASSED BY THE TIME SIENA MET RODERICK in the great hall. A kitchen servant passed her as she scurried out of the room not bothering to greet Siena. It appeared Roderick was putting something into a bag. He closed the bag and looked up as she approached. "Are ye ready to leave, lass?"

"Should I have Agatha get ready to go?"

"Nay, lass. We will not be gone long."

Siena decided not to argue since she was a guest in his home, and it would save Agatha from going out into the wintery weather. "Let me retrieve my cloak."

In no time, Siena was back wrapped in her purple cloak. Roderick handed her his plaid.

"I don't understand," Siena said. "What do I do with it?"

He took the plaid and wrapped it around her shoulders and then tossed the remainder over her left shoulder. "There. 'Tis verra cold outside and snowin'. Nothing like a plaid to keep ye warm."

"Should we wait and go another time?"

"Nay." He picked up the bag and headed toward the door.

Siena wondered if Roderick was a man of few words. He sure hadn't used many around her, and she had no idea what he was thinking or how he felt. Nevertheless, she followed him outside like an obedient puppy. An icy breath of fresh air hit her in the face. She gasped.

Good Lord, it had gotten colder.

Garvin had brought their mounts up to the front steps, so they wouldn't have to walk to the stables. Roderick's horse stood still while Star was dancing around impatient to leave.

"I think yer horse is ready to stretch her legs, lass," Garvin said as he helped Siena to mount.

"Thank you, Garvin," Siena tightened her hold on the reins. "She is a bit frisky today. Perhaps she is trying to stay warm."

Garvin chuckled.

Once Roderick had mounted, he looked at her and asked, "Now lass which cave did you take Michael to? We have three different caves for safety."

"It was the one in the hill off the main road. Your wife told me about it as I had not remembered seeing a cave when I came."

"It will be easy enough to get to and we can return before the weather turns too bad. Ye can ride, can't ye? I've not actually seen ye on yer own horse."

Siena frowned at him. "Of course, I can ride." It was one of the few things she'd taken pleasure in doing back home.

Roderick raised a brow in question. The man seemed to have little faith in her abilities, and she wondered if the icy air wasn't hitting him in the face like it was hers. He acted like it was a mild summer's day and they were going for a ride in the country.

Roderick turned and led the way out of the castle. They cantered down the road until they came to a cave carved into a huge dirt mound. No one would ever guess that it was anything but a hill the way they had disguised it. The entrance had loose brush that looked like bushes in front of the opening.

Roderick dismounted and pulled the brush out of the way and sat them to the left of the opening. Next, he helped Siena dismount. They led their horses into the mouth of the cave, so they would not be out in the stormy weather. There was plenty of room for them and there was straw on the ground indicating this was where animals were kept.

"This is a most unusual cave," Siena commented as she unwrapped the plaid and shook off the snow. She watched Roderick strike a flint. He held it to one of the torches until it burned bright orange. Next, he lit the other four torches that were in metal brackets along the wall.

"We made the cave ourselves. As ye can see, it is well supported with timbers and supplies for anyone who would have to stay here. He grabbed one of the torches and lit the pile of wood that was already stacked in a stone circle located in the middle of the cave. She watched the white smoke spiral up and out an opening that had been made in the roof so that the cave wouldn't become smoky.

"The pit is for warmth?" she asked.

"Aye. We built it to hide our women, so they would be safe

during an unexpected raid. Unfortunately for us, it dinna work when yer brother attacked."

"I wonder why they didn't use it?"

Roderick shook his head. "I dinna ken. It appeared that a few women were on the road headed toward the caves when they were struck down and left for dead. 'Twas the way we found them."

"I'm so sorry," she said. It was no wonder Roderick was bitter. She would be too.

Siena wandered to the back of the cave where there were two very large, square timbers stacked on the floor. "This is where I left Michael." She knelt down and looked around the dirt floor. Spotting a small gray stone, she picked it up. It was cool and smooth to the touch.

"Do ye remember anything?"

"No." She shook her head. "Elen said if I'd find a small stone and keep turning it over and over in my hand that maybe I could see something. You have to remember that I'm still new at being a seer."

"I dinna imagine these things can be forced. We'll give it some time." He spread a tartan out and motioned for her to join him by the fire. He liked the sound of her voice ... it was soft, pleasant and English. He smiled at the thought. Who would have thought that he'd like anything English?

The timbers behind them had been draped with furs for softness, and now they had fire in front, which gave warmth from the chilly air outside.

"Did ye light a torch for Michael?"

"I did long enough to get him settled, but I put it out when I left. I was afraid someone would see the light. I did tell him his mother would be along shortly so not to be afraid. He had his favorite stuffed rabbit."

"Ah," Roderick nodded. "Michael is afraid of the dark."

Siena noticed that he didn't speak as if he thought his son was dead. "I'm sorry. I didn't know, but I'd hoped his mother would be along shortly with the other women, and he wouldn't be alone. I'm sure I warned your wife that there wasn't much time."

"'Tis not yer fault, lass." He extended his hand out toward her. "Let me see the *creag*."

"It is nothing special." She handed him the stone that she'd been turning over and over in her hand. For just the briefest moment, their skin touched, and she felt the oddest reaction. As if she'd come alive for the first time. It gave her warmth inside.

Roderick took the warm stone and held it in his fist. *If only the stone would work.* He'd never believed in any kind of magic. Now he was desperate. "I dinna see how this *creag* will do anythin'." He dropped it back in her hand.

"I don't know either. She caught the stone then glanced toward the opening. "Is that rain? It sounds funny."

Roderick stood, then walked to the cave opening. He held his hand out in the snow. "Nay, lass, worse. It's sleet. If it keeps up, we'll have to spend the night. I dinna think that we would have sleet today or we wouldna have ridden out." He ran his hands through his hair. We could make a dash toward the castle, but I'm still hoping ye'll see somethin'. 'Tis all downhill and we dinna want to endanger our mounts. I'd rather wait. Let's hope it snows over the sleet tonight which will make it easier goin' tomorrow."

Alone with Roderick … it was highly improper, but she'd spent so much time with him that she didn't feel strange.

Because he'd been so kind to her, and she had no fear of him. "Will your men worry?"

Roderick glanced at her like she had just insulted him, then he said, "I think I can protect us, lass. Besides we can see the castle from here, so I'm no worried about attacks."

He went outside and retrieved a small barrel, which he dragged inside. Withdrawing a dirk from his sock, he broke the ice, so the animals would have something to drink. Next, he unsaddled both animals and gave them some feed that was stored in a barrel in the corner of the cave.

"I must say you have this place well prepared, even food for the animals," Siena said as she started to get to her feet. "Can I help you do something?"

"Nay, lass." He pulled a torch out of a bracket and went to the mouth of the cave. He waved it several times before putting it back into place. Then he strolled back over to her with a sack in his hand, which he dropped on the blanket.

"Why did you do that?"

"I was afraid something like this might happen. The torch was a signal to let my guards ken we are spendin' the night." He smiled at her. "Remember, I am with the White Witch."

Siena straightened and gasped. "I don't believe you said that."

Roderick grinned. She saw such a different man than the more serious one she'd seen before, and he was quite handsome with a square jaw and a hint of dimple in his left cheek.

She couldn't believe he was actually joking with her. Well two could play at the game. "Then you best remember, my lord, I am a White Witch, so you could leave this cave as a toad."

Roderick threw back his head and laughed. A sound Siena found very appealing.

"I brought some bannocks and cheese in case we were stuck here. But we'll have to share the whisky. It will help keep us warm. Ye do drink whisky?"

"I'm afraid not."

"Ye'll be in for a treat then."

After he placed a couple of logs on the fire, Roderick joined her, and they leaned back against the furs that covered the timbers and began to eat.

Siena pinched off a piece of bread. It hung in her throat, so she waved her hand and pointed to her throat. Roderick handed her his pouch and she took a big swallow of whisky which burned her throat all the way down. She began to cough, so Roderick patted her on the back.

"It takes some gettin' used to, lass."

"It sure does. It is different from ale." She wiped the tears from her eyes. "W--why don't you tell me a little bit about your family? The more I know the sooner I can help you."

Roderick would have normally refused. He didn't like talking about himself, but he'd had several healthy sips of whisky and he was a bit more relaxed. "Let me see. I have four younger brothers, Galen, Gillard, Patrick, and Angus. My parents died several years ago in a fire. Since I'm the oldest, I became laird, however, my brothers are verra independent and they set up their own holdings. All just a stone's throw from here."

"I'm sorry about your parents."

"I was too. They were fine people, but sometime accidents happen, and we have no control over them. Being the oldest, I had to step in and take over the clan at a young age."

"That must have been hard."

"Aye, it makes a mon of ye fast."

"Were you and Gillian married long?"

"Five years. My wife and I grew up together, so it was a natural thing to wed." He sighed. "She was a good woman and a good mother who died much too young." Roderick frowned over his memories. "Enough about me. Tell me somethin' about yerself."

"There isn't much to tell. I've never done anything exciting or traveled anywhere." Siena hated talking about her life when she only wanted to forget it, however, as she rolled the stones together in her pocket, a peace came over her and she began to relax. "I was born a twin, but my mother and brother died at my birth, which some have blamed on me." She took a sip of whisky and sighed. "Like a baby could do something like that."

"Nonsense."

"Nevertheless, my older brother, who was a good fifteen years older than me, helped fuel the rumors, and said the devil had marked me." She stuck out her arm. "See. I hate it. I try to keep it hidden because I do feel marked."

Roderick rubbed his thumb over the strange mark and something deep inside him stirred. Was it only compassion or something more? He wasn't sure. He'd been so full of hate these last few years that there had been little room for anything else, but now he found he wanted to comfort Siena. He wanted to erase the hurt he saw in her eyes. "'Tis a birthmark nothing more, lass."

"Thank you. But others feel differently." Siena stared at him for a moment before she spoke again. "If I hadn't had Agatha, I'm not sure what I would have done. She managed to get Father John to teach me to read and write and that helped keep my mind busy. When I got older my father sent me to live with Fidach."

"What happened to yer father?"

"He's still alive so I guess I do have a relative, but I've not seen him in several years."

"Yet, he sent ye to yer brother?"

"He did. I think seeing me reminded him of my mother," she paused as if she were lost in the past. "Strange. I never remember being held by my father." She shrugged, then continued. "Fidach was happy having me, torturing me became his favorite pastime."

What a horrible childhood Siena had, Roderick thought. He clenched his fist. "What would he do?"

"Lock me in a dark room and leave me there. Once it took Agatha two days to find me –" she trailed off with a faraway look in her eyes. "By the time she did, I was hoarse from screaming."

Roderick was so angry that he wanted to kill Fidach all over again. Yet he didn't want to scare Siena, so he kept a tight hold on his emotions. This young woman had known little love in her lifetime and his heart swelled with a feeling he thought long dead. He touched her arm. Siena turned to him with tear-filled eyes.

Roderick pulled Siena over to him and enfolded her in his arms. "I'm so sorry, lass. Ye will not have to go through something like that ever again. Ye dinna have to say any more."

"Maybe it will do me good to get it all out," she said, her head still on his chest. "On the last day at Berwick, Fidach had been in a rage about you. He'd already hit me twice that day, but when he grabbed me for the third time, I came up with a knife. I sunk it deep into his heart," she paused, then added softly, "I should feel sorry for taking a life, but I don't."

Roderick pushed her long hair over her shoulder and wiped

the tears from her cheeks with his thumb. "Sometimes men are evil and there is no good in them. I believe yer brother was such a mon and deserved to die."

Siena raised up and looked at him, then said, "Thank you." Roderick might be a fierce warrior, but he was being so tender with her that her heart was melting. What would it be like to be kissed by such a man? She felt a warmth creep through her veins, and she longed for something more.

Roderick cradled her in the crook of his arm and lowered his mouth to hers. His lips were wonderful, warm, teasing. His fingers slid to the back of her neck as his lips moved against hers. She could taste whisky on Roderick's lips, and when he coaxed her lips apart, she gasped as his tongue dove into her mouth. Siena had never felt this way before and she had surely never experienced a man's kiss. She found she liked the way he kissed her. A liquid fire burned in her blood like the hottest fire, clouding her brain. Her desire for him overrode everything else.

Siena's arms slid around his neck and she began to explore his mouth as he had hers. She heard his moan which sounded more like a growl, so she leaned back, thinking she'd done something wrong. "I--I'm so sorry." Perhaps, she wasn't good at this thing called kissing.

Pulling her back to him, he held her tight, and kissed the side of her neck. "Ye did nothing wrong, lass. 'Tis I who should apologize." Roderick waited for his breathing to return to normal. He didn't know what it was about this slip of a woman, but she had touched him deep down. "Know this … no one will ever hurt ye again. Ye have my promise." And with a supreme effort, Roderick ignored the urge to make love to her, he finally said, "We better get some sleep." He pulled her beside him and said no more.

Siena felt someone truly cared for her … maybe not love … but actually cared what happened to her. She knew there was something special about this man from the very beginning. Roderick had awakened something within her, and it left her reeling, but also contented.

A strange feeling.

For the first time in her life Siena felt safe because she trusted Roderick completely.

CHAPTER 9

"*L*aird Scott, the road has been cleared for ye!"

Duncan's booming voice jarred Siena awake from the peaceful dream she'd been having. She had to blink several times before she could focus. That is when she realized she was half laying on top of Roderick. Perhaps, she'd never been exposed to men much in her life, but she knew this was no lady-like position, so she scrambled to put some distance between them. What must Duncan think of her? Surely, he couldn't see them from the mouth of the cave. Better yet, what must Roderick think of a woman sleeping with him whom he wasn't married to? She didn't like the answer to her question.

Roderick sat up and spoke, "I thank ye for yer concern, Duncan, but I'm sure we could huv made our way home this mornin'."

"We must take care of our laird. Can I speak with ye for a moment?" Duncan asked. He'd only taken a step into the cave, but he thought better about it and turned to wait outside for Roderick.

"Sorry for the interruption, lass."

Siena nodded not knowing what to say, but she was sure her eyes must have been huge with embarrassment.

Roderick shoved himself to his feet and stretched before making his way to the mouth of the cave. "What is it?" he snapped. "It had better be good. 'Twas the first good night's sleep I've had in a while."

Duncan noticed the mon did have on his clothes. "So that's what ye were doin'?"

"I dinna care for yer insolence, Duncan."

"Weel I dinna think ye realize that ye have put the lass's reputation in question."

They stood right outside the mouth of the cave, so Siena wouldn't be able to hear them. "What the hell are ye talking about, Duncan?"

"It dinna go unnoticed that ye and the lass dinna return last night."

"And?"

"Now the men think the White Witch has cast a spell on ye and ye might not be right in the head." Duncan took a step back as he said this. Just in case Roderick decided to swing at him.

"By all that's holy!" Roderick did swing, but his arms flew up instead of at Duncan. "Such nonsense. Do ye not have anythin' better to do but gossip? I need to find my son, and Lady Siena, if she has any special powers, is going to help."

"Ye dinna have to shout. I'm standing right in front of ye."

"Ah, wull, be glad that yer not picking yer arse off the ground."

"Ouch." Duncan stood a little straighter. "Someone needs to

be telling ye. Ye'll go back and someone might try and hurt the lass. Do ye want that?"

"They will do no such thing!" Roderick turned back to the cave. "Be off. We will follow shortly."

Laird Scott didn't look happy when he came back to where Siena sat. He stood with his hands on his hips, but he didn't say anything, and she had no idea what he was thinking. Had she crossed some line and was in trouble?

When he didn't speak, she finally asked, "Is something wrong?"

Roderick appeared to have been in a daze, because his eyes sharpened and now, he was looking at her when he asked, "What makes ye say that?"

"You don't look exactly happy, and I heard you shout, so I figured I must have done something wrong."

"Ah, wull not ye, lass." Roderick shook his head. "'Twas I who forgot ye were a lady."

"I think you have insulted me, but I'm not sure."

"Nay," he said, shaking his head. "But ye *are* a lady and shouldn't have spent the night with me. Yer reputation is now ruined."

Siena started laughing. "I hate to tell you, but my reputation wasn't too good at home, but for a different reason. I'm not sure that I've ever been a proper lady because I've lived such a sheltered life, but I thank you for your concern."

Roderick chuckled. "This is different and all my fault. We shall marry." The words were out of his mouth before he realized that he'd said them. He couldn't believe what he'd just said, however, the look of astonishment on Siena's face made Roderick want to smile again. Apparently, he'd shocked her. And he had most certainly shocked himself.

"You want me to marry you?"

"Aye."

She had a doubtful look in her eyes. "You are not very good at proposing," Siena told him.

"'Tis not every day that I ask someone to marry me, lass." Hell, he never thought he would utter those words again in his lifetime.

"But you didn't ask me."

"Ye will marry me lass and be under my protection. I command it."

"You cannot command someone to marry you."

"Aye, I can." He looked smug as he rocked back on his heels.

"But we don't know each other very well."

"People have started with less." He extended his hand down to her. "Let's go back to Black Dawn and make the announcement."

Siena took his hand and stood. "Are you sure you want to do this?" She saw a sparkle in his eyes, and before she knew what was happening, Roderick had jerked her into his arms and kissed her. Not a gentle kiss. It was more like he was branding her. The demanding kiss robbed Siena of her breath. His tongue sank into her mouth and she felt the intimacy as she returned his kiss. She was so shocked at her own eager response that she couldn't think, blood pounded in her brain and made her knees tremble. The kiss was exhilarating, making her want to get closer to him.

Suddenly, he lifted her away from him. The cold air quickly replaced the warmth of his body, and she knew she had a startled expression.

"Ye will marry me."

"As you wish, milord," Siena murmured, knowing at this

very moment she couldn't deny him anything. There was something about Roderick that pulled at her, and she liked these new feelings.

"Obedience. I like that," Roderick chuckled.

ONCE THEY HAD MOUNTED, SIENA NOTICED THAT THE ROAD WAS just a small rut to the castle and it appeared to have iced again, so she rubbed the stones together and wished for an open road to the castle. When she opened her eyes, sure enough the road was clear with the ice pushed to the side, so the horses had a perfect path.

"I wonder how long it took Duncan to clear the road?" Roderick more or less said this to himself. "Must have taken all night."

Siena smiled. "They did a good job. They must have been worried about you."

"Aye." Roderick nodded, but still shook his head because the road appeared to never have seen the first drop of ice.

As they entered through the gates the clan started to gather. Siena wondered if someone was going to throw a stone her way because they really didn't look happy. She wondered if they all thought she'd seduced their laird. If they thought that, then they didn't know him very well.

Once they stopped just outside the great hall, Roderick dismounted, then helped her down. He guided her to the steps before he turned to address the crowd. He kept his arm around her.

"I will be marrying Lady Siena in three days hence. Know ye this, she did us all a great favor when she killed our enemy,

Fidach, so she avenged our loss. Now, Lady Siena is going to be a member of Clan Scott, and I expect everyone to welcome her."

"She bewitched you, laird," someone called out.

"Nay, she did not. I'm the same mon I was the day before. Put such thoughts from yer head."

Siena watched everyone nod. She wished he'd said that he loved her and that was the reason for the wedding, instead it was as if he were repaying a debt, and nothing more. However, she wanted more and somehow, she would find a way to make Roderick love her.

They turned and stepped into the entrance that led into the great hall. "I bid ye good day, lass." Roderick excused himself to attend to more important matters, leaving Siena to wonder if she was doing the right thing. Did they have to post bans in Scotland? She wasn't sure.

She didn't know … she didn't know anything. Everything was happening much too fast. Her reaction to Roderick confused her. And then she thought what other choice did she have? She liked the safe feeling she had here with him, and though she didn't want to admit it … she liked Roderick.

Siena climbed the stairs in a daze. Agatha waited at the top for her.

"Where have you been?" Agatha asked. At the moment, she reminded Siena of an angry cat with its hair standing up on its back. "I was worried sick about you, milady."

"I'm sorry to have worried you, but it wasn't my fault, so you can calm down." Siena took a breath, then continued, "I went to the cave with Laird Scott."

"Aye, I knew that." Agatha threw her hands up in the air. "But you didn't come back."

Siena swept by Agatha and headed to her solar, but she said

over her shoulder, "The weather changed and turned into sleet, so we couldn't risk the horses falling and breaking a leg."

Agatha was dead on Siena's heels. "You spent the night with the laird?"

Siena felt like a child. Agatha had been the only one to ever discipline her, so Siena remembered all the lectures. She really couldn't think of anything to say so she nodded as they entered her chamber.

"Oh, my Lord. I need to sit down," Agatha held her chest as if she were in pain and stumbled over to a chair by the window to take a seat.

Siena poured a cup of cool water and handed it to Agatha. "Drink this and calm down. Don't go getting out of sorts. Nothing happened," Siena said as she sat on the bed and shoved her hair over her shoulders.

"I should hope not. I raised you better than that, but you know you shouldn't be alone with a man without a chaperone."

"Yes. I should be hung." She smiled at her own joke. "I guess you didn't hear the announcement that was made just now?"

"What announcement?" Agatha set her cup down. "I've been mending a couple of your dresses."

"I'm getting married. Roderick just made the announcement."

Agatha gasped again, and then a slow smile formed on her lips. "My baby girl is getting married." She sighed. "Now that is good news."

"But I don't know how to be a wife. I don't know how to run a home."

"Then you shall learn, milady."

THE NEXT THREE DAYS BECAME A BLUR TO SIENA.

Siena and Agatha walked over to see the church. It wasn't a very big chapel, but it had a quaint feel to it that Siena liked. There were ten rows of benches on each side and they had the Scott red plaid on the floor leading to the altar. Surely, she could make the short walk down the aisle without fainting and making a fool of herself.

As they left to go back to the main holding, Siena turned the small stones over and over in her fingers. It was a habit she was developing when she was thinking. "I wish there would be flowers in the church."

"If you were getting married in the spring that might be possible but with this frozen ground nothing could live," Agatha commented.

"I know but still …."

SIENA FELT LIKE SHE WAS GOING TO ANOTHER HANGING, AND THIS time there would be no one to save her. Then she would think 'save her from what?' She actually cared for Roderick. There was no denying that he was nice to look upon, and he had been good to her. So why, couldn't she be happy?

Because he didn't love her. She hadn't seen that spark in his eyes that told her of his love, and so far. he sure hadn't mentioned the word. The only thing he felt was the need to protect her with marriage. Well marriage would certainly do that and there could be no greater champion than Roderick, but she wanted love. For once in her life, she needed someone to love her.

Her mind was whirling when Agatha entered with Siena's gown.

"Are you pacing again, milady?" Agatha placed the gown on the bed and smoothed the skirt with her hands.

"I feel so restless, Agatha." Siena was wringing her hands. "I'm going to throw up."

"All brides feel that way on their wedding day. It isn't unusual."

"You mean everyone wants to throw up?"

Agatha chuckled. "Something like that. It is a big step, but I do believe that it will be good for you. From this day forward, you will be protected."

"I know. But what if I'm expected to . . . well you know." Siena felt her cheeks grow warm. "I don't know what to do."

Agatha smiled. "Don't fret, milady. Believe it or not it will come to you. Remember when you first learned how to ride a horse?"

Siena nodded.

"You were afraid until you got the hang of it and then you thought riding was wonderful. It is just that simple."

Siena gave her a doubtful look. "But I still don't know what to do."

"Your husband will show you. You just have to trust him. He will not hurt you."

"Are you sure?"

"Aye. I remember my Robert when he was alive," Agatha sighed, locked in a long-ago memory. "By the way, the laird's brothers have arrived this morning, so you will be meeting his family today."

"Have you seen them?"

"Just a glimpse. They are fine-looking huge men. Perhaps

not as handsome as our laird, but I wouldn't turn any of them down." Agatha's face turned a lovely shade of red.

"Agatha! I've never heard you talk like that." Siena laughed. She felt all the tension leave her body, seeping away like water going to sea, and she finally felt calm.

"I have something for you," Agatha said before she disappeared into the solar. It was only a couple of seconds before she returned with a small cup of whisky. "Here drink this. It will help with your nerves."

"Thank you." Siena sipped the whisky, feeling that slow burn down her throat. "It isn't bad."

"Let's get you dressed." Agatha motioned for Siena to come over to her. "We have taken one of your dresses and redesigned it. I wanted it to be fancy for your wedding. I think you will look lovely in this gown."

Siena slipped on her hose and then her kirtle. Next came the cotehardie which was emerald green velvet. It had large sleeves that had been trimmed in gold. Next, Agatha had Siena sit upon a chair, so she could pull her hair up in curls which spilled over her shoulders.

"You look so pretty, milady," Agatha said once she'd finished. "Let's go downstairs. I believe everyone is waiting in the chapel for you."

CHAPTER 10

*O*nce outside, the church was to the left of the keep.

Two trees flanked either side of the building as if they offered protection to the church which was made of the same stone as the keep. A set of double red doors greeted all who entered. The red was to keep the devil out.

Siena hadn't paid much attention to the small building when she'd been out before, but now she had to admit it was lovely sitting nestled in the snow. The sky was a brilliant blue with not a cloud in the sky. It was a beautiful day for a wedding. Her wedding. She still couldn't believe she was getting married.

A noise caught her attention and she looked over her shoulder and found clansmen walking up the hill. What was their mood? Thankfully, she would enter the church before they gathered just in case they wanted to throw stones.

Agatha held Siena's gown up so that it would not drag in the snow and wet mud where others had walked back and forth, creating a sloppy mess. Once they entered the vestibule, Agatha helped straighten Siena's gown.

"You are ready, milady," Agatha said as she smoothed her hand across the dress once more.

"What if this is some kind of sick joke and Roderick is not inside the church standing by the altar waiting for me? I've not seen him in a couple of days. He could have changed his mind."

"There. There." Agatha hugged Siena. "You're nervous as all brides are before they are married. It is only natural. Take some deep breaths." Agatha patted Siena's back as she tried to control her breathing. I'll go inside and sit down and then you are to enter. If Roderick isn't there, then I'll come back out and we can leave."

"Thank you," Siena murmured as Agatha walked away. Siena waited and held her breath, slowly she let out her breath. It seemed like forever before she got up the nerve to shove the door open and enter the church. What had she told herself before? She was finished being afraid of everything. She was a strong woman . . . she hoped.

Siena gasped. She couldn't believe what she was seeing. The church was filled with red and white roses. Sprays of flowers were on each pew and the altar was covered in blood red roses. Her wish had come true.

All heads turned toward her. Siena hoped she managed a small smile as she held her head high and took the first step to a new life with a man she hardly knew. Her legs were a little wobbly as she moved down the aisle.

When Roderick turned toward her, she noticed that his brothers stood beside him. They were all huge, strapping men. Roderick was maybe a couple of inches taller, but they all had those piercing black eyes. However, it was Roderick's gaze that held her and kept her moving forward instead of running back out the door. Today he was especially handsome dressed in a white shirt and his red kilt. His crimson tartan swept from his right shoulder in a graceful drape. His silver crest stood out. A stag trippant encircled in a leather strap inscribed with the clan's motto *"Amo"*. She'd found out that meant *I love*.

When she neared the altar, she took Roderick's warm hand. He squeezed her cold fingers as they turned and faced the priest who motioned for them to kneel.

Roderick felt like he'd been punched in the stomach. His little mouse now looked like a beautiful woman. Her skin glowed in the candlelight and her eyes glistened silver as did her long black hair. A surge of warmth soared over him. He'd kept his emotions under control for so long that the surge of warmth that swept over him once he saw Siena was bewildering. And bewildering wasn't something he cared for. He liked control, but he had to admit at the moment he felt wonderful.

The priest after saying a prayer asked for the ring, which brought Roderick back to the moment. He turned to Galen who placed their mother's ring in Roderick's palm.

Father Collins took the ring from Roderick and blessed it, then he said, "Place the ring on the fourth finger."

Roderick first placed the ring on her thumb and said, "In the name of the Father." Then he moved the ring on her index finger and said, "And of the Son." Next was her middle finger. "And the Holy Ghost." Last was her fourth finger as he said, "With this ring, I thee wed."

Siena nodded as she looked at the large ruby that twinkled up at her. The stone was breathtakingly beautiful and large. She wondered if it had belonged to Roderick's first wife.

Siena was actually glad she wasn't required to say anything.

She would probably croak like a frog because at the moment everything seemed surreal. However, she did have to repeat her vows and her voice shook, but she got through them.

Then before she knew what was happening, she caught a flash of silver out of the corner of her eye and her wrist was cut.

"Ooww," Siena cried as she jerked back her arm and stared at the thin line of bright red blood.

"Trust me," Roderick whispered. "'Tis part of the ceremony."

She frowned at him, thinking this was a strange custom.

Next, he cut his wrist, and then placed it over her cut so that their blood mixed. And in that very brief moment, Siena saw glimpses of Roderick's son, Michael, and it gave her hope that the child lived.

A small white strip of cloth was placed around both their hands.

"Our blood has been mixed. Yer blood is mine and my blood is yours until the end of time."

Siena was so touched that tears sprang to her eyes. *They were one*, she thought. Maybe this was a good custom after all. She hoped this meant Roderick couldn't get rid of her. "You promise?" she whispered.

Roderick nodded with a slight smile.

The priest kissed Roderick's cheek, then announced, "The kiss of peace." Roderick in turn kissed Siena briefly on the lips before he turned her to face the congregation. There were whoops of Scottish enthusiasm.

Later Siena would think that she didn't remember anything about the ceremony other than the cut on the wrist, and that she did remember. All she had to do was look at her wrist with the linen tied around the cut to remember.

Once they were outside of the church, they stopped so

Roderick could address the clan. "May I present, Lady Siena Scott. You shall pledge yer loyalty to her as ye have to me." Everyone cheered. "Then let the feasting begin."

Siena glanced up at her husband and she felt the blackness closing in around her as heat made her skin feel hot, and everything was swimming. She vaguely remembered being draped across Roderick's arm. She could hear what was going on, but she couldn't respond.

"I see ye've swept your bride off her feet," Angus said with a chuckle.

"Aye, it appears the lass is overcome with emotion and she has fainted."

"Wull, if I am marrying yer sorry ass … I'd faint, too," Galen added.

Roderick frowned at his brothers before he scooping his bride up in his arms and heading toward the keep. Evidently, he'd overwhelmed his bride. He hoped it was a good sign.

Siena felt terrible when she came to. Agatha was holding a cool cloth to her head.

"What happened?" Siena asked, blinking with bafflement.

"You fainted, milady."

She sat up. "How embarrassing."

"It is probably lack of food, and you were a bit nervous. Do you think you can join everyone for the celebration?"

"I think I'm good now. If I go down again just leave me," she said with a laugh as she experienced a gamut of perplexing emotions.

The door opened and The Green Lady swept into the room.

"I came to see if I could help," Elen said.

"I'm not sure why I fainted but I'm feeling better … maybe a little weak.

"Drink this," Elen said as she dug into her pouch and brought out a very small, brown bottle.

Siena reached for it. "What is it?"

"Just a few herbs that will make ye feel better. I take it myself. When ye are hundred and sixteen, ye need something to keep you movin'."

Siena drank the potion. "It does taste good."

"Aye." Elen nodded. "Now it's time to join the celebration. "We've waited a long time to see our Laird happy again." She swept out the door.

"I thought she was hundred and five," Agatha said.

Siena laughed. "I don't think she knows her real age."

THE FEAST IN THE GREAT HALL WAS ELABORATE. THE TABLES HAD been pushed to the sides of the walls, leaving a place in the middle so people could dance. The tables were filled with not only guards but also clansmen and women as everyone had been invited. They were all talking and laughing among themselves.

There was some kind of dancing going on in the middle of the floor and was accompanied by bagpipes, but it was not a dance that Siena could identify. However, it looked like fun because everyone was laughing and clapping.

Siena and Roderick were seated in the middle of the high table with Roderick's brothers on either side of them.

Galen, the youngest brother sat next to her. He was like a younger version of Roderick, but now that she could see him up close, she noticed Galen's eyes were hazel.

"I guess I should welcome ye to the family," Galen said with a smile, then added, "That is if my brother would introduce us."

Siena could tell Galen wasn't as serious as his brothers. He actually smiled at her and there was a wicked twinkle in his eyes and adorable dimples.

Roderick peered around her. His brow arched. "Siena, let me introduce ye to my youngest brother, Galen, who always seems to be in a hurry to get anything done. Somehow, we never have been able to teach him patience." Roderick nodded to his left. "On his other side is Angus, he is next to the oldest, and supposedly has the wisdom of the family."

"And wiser," Angus said with a grin. "'Tis nice to meet you, lass."

"On my side is Gillard who is stubborn and Patrick who is very resourceful.

"And as ye ken, our brother claims to have all of these traits," Patrick said. "He thinks he is perfect."

They all laughed.

"'Twould have been nicer if we had met ye before the weddin'," Galen grumbled.

"I don't think there was time," Siena said.

"My God, she's a Sassenach!" Gillard bellowed, having recognized her accent.

Siena brow arched. "I take it you have a problem with me being English?"

"Everyone kens we have no love for England," Patrick said. "They try to rule us in everything we do."

"I believe ye missed it today, when Siena said yes to me and she became a Scott like the rest of ye," Rodrick pointed out.

"That's true," Gillard said.

"Well," Siena said, drawing everyone's attention. "I believe you should judge the person and not by where they were born."

All the brothers laughed, then Galen said, "I see the lass has a mind of her own."

"Aye, she does," Roderick agreed and squeezed her hand under the table.

"Did ye hear?" Angus asked Roderick. "Those damn Elliot's stole some of our coos."

"'Tis not the first time. They can no seem to remember where their borders are located and probably need remindin'," Roderick said. "What's the plan?"

"We're going to take them back," Angus said. "Ye interested?"

"Aye." All the brothers chimed in.

While the men talked and made plans, Siena ate her dinner. The roasted chicken was perfect for her empty stomach. She watched the crowd who seemed to be having a grand time, then she spotted Agatha who was dancing with Duncan. Since Agatha didn't know the steps Duncan was laughing and swinging her round and round.

Agatha appeared so much younger than she normally did. Maybe she was happy at long last, thought Siena. Agatha hadn't had it easy when they lived at Berwick castle. Siena's brother had been just as mean to Agatha especially when she tried to protect her.

Siena reached for her cup and took a sip of the delicious red wine. A room flashed before her face and she glimpsed a small church near Edinburgh. Just as suddenly the great hall had replaced her vision leaving her puzzled as to what she had just seen.

"Are ye all right?" Roderick asked.

Slowly Siena turned to him as she tried to calm her racing heart. Evidently, she had gasped, drawing his attention.

"I—I'm fine. Perhaps a little tired."

"Why dinna ye go ahead and retire for the night, lass. I'm sure everyone will understand."

Siena nodded then rose to her feet. She bid the brothers good night.

"I'll help her," Galen said as he started to get up.

"No ye won't," Roderick said with a stern glance.

"I'm fine, Galen, thank you," she told him.

As Siena made her way from the room she wondered if she would be all right. Now that she knew the secret.

A secret that men would kill to have.

A secret that would remain guarded until a time that she needed it.

CHAPTER 11

Siena was glad that she'd had Agatha move her things to the laird's solar. She opened the door and surveyed her new room. She took a deep breath and tucked her secret safely in the back of her mind.

The laird's bedroom was much larger than the room she had been in and the bed appeared huge with its four posters. There were no hangings around the bed as she once had on hers back home. It was plain and masculine with the red tartan spread across the foot.

A rug that extended all around the bed, felt plush when she stepped on it. There wasn't a lot of furniture, but she did see a chest at the end of the bed and several more chests on one wall with hooks above them. Two chairs flanked a round table in front of the fireplace and she thought that would be a nice place to do needlework because there were two windows instead of one so there would be plenty of light to see by.

However, what caught her eye now was her white nightgown that had been draped across the red plaid bedcovers. She felt a chill run up her arms. She didn't think it was possible to be scared and thrilled at the same time but that is how she would describe the butterflies in her stomach. She didn't waste any time changing into her gown, then climbed into bed. She would be very uncomfortable if she'd had to undress in front of Roderick.

What if Roderick wasn't pleased that she had no idea what she was supposed to do? What if he didn't like the way she looked? She started breathing quickly. She needed to calm down she reminded herself or she'd faint again and that would never do.

This could be a short marriage.

RODERICK OPENED THE DOOR.

He glanced around the room until he spotted Siena, then he shut the door behind him and bolted the door. He didn't move but stood there staring at her and taking her breath away. Roderick seemed to fill the doorway with his broad shoulders and those piercing black eyes. How could she be so lucky?

Siena straightened her shoulders as she leaned back on the pillows, wondering what he was thinking. Should she be doing something? He definitely wasn't smiling at the moment. Could he possibly be regretting the marriage already? My God she was a bundle of nerves as she gripped the bedding.

"Ye know, lass," Roderick shoved away from the wall and moved toward the chairs. "I never thought to see someone in my bed again." He sat down on the brown chair and pulled off his boots.

"A--Any regrets?"

Roderick jerked his head back to her. "Nay, lass. Yer so beautiful, I feel like a very lucky mon." He saw doubt in Siena's eyes. She appeared frightened. "Ye dinna believe me?"

"I-I've never had anyone tell me I was beautiful, but Agatha, and she is more or less required to say nice things," Siena said with a smile.

Roderick chuckled as he continued to undress. He tossed his shirt over the back of the chair. "All ye have to do is look in a mirror to see that I tell the truth."

"I was never allowed a mirror when I went to live with my brother. Besides it's a sin to dwell on one's appearance."

"Then ye'll have to take my word, lass." He unbuckled his belt and his kilt fell to the floor, causing Siena to gasp.

Her intake of breath told him that he would have to take things slow. She looked like she could bolt at any minute the way she had her hands gripping the sheets. "Ye dinna need to be afraid of me, lass," he said in a soft voice.

Good Lord Almighty, Siena thought.

She couldn't help peeking between her fingers as he dropped his kilt on the chair by the fireplace. His body was so muscular and strong. She didn't think there was an ounce of fat on his body. And he ... he was so big. She didn't see how their bodies would ever fit together. When he turned back toward her, she lowered her gaze, feeling shy and unsure of herself. She wondered for a moment if they could just be friends.

The bed sagged as Roderick slid under the covers. The next thing Siena knew she was being pulled over next to his warm body. He slipped a finger under her chin and tilted her face up to him. She gazed into his dark eyes unsure of what to say or do. She wished she'd had a mother to tell her what she was expected to do as a wife.

"Dinna be afraid."

"I'm not afraid of you," she said, ignoring the mocking voice inside of her that wondered why he'd chosen her. "I-It's just that . . . I'm unsure what I'm supposed to do."

"Ah," Roderick said as he rubbed his hand up and down her arm. "I think we should take this slow for now. I'll teach ye everythin' ye need to know. Ye just have to trust me. This is one time that I'm verra glad ye have had no experience."

"I want to be a proper wife."

"And ye shall be," Roderick murmured as he lowered his mouth and kissed her neck. Siena was magnificent. He felt her tense the minute he touched her neck before relaxing as her hands slid behind his head. Her skin felt like velvet. He rubbed his hand down her back.

His decision was made . . . no matter how badly he wanted Siena, he was going to teach her desire before he mated with her . . . even if it killed him. He braced his arms to support his weight so that he didn't crush her.

Siena moaned as Roderick placed feather-like kisses on her neck. And then he was kissing her ear which sent heat to her private parts. She squirmed. She didn't know something like this could feel so wonderful as he shifted until his lips were touching hers. The kiss was surprisingly gentle at first and then he applied pressure to her lips. When she opened her mouth to complain, he took advantage and plunged his tongue deep inside, producing a shock wave through her entire body and a moan that sounded more like a squeal as it escaped her lips.

Lord, this had to be sinful, she thought as his hand curved around her neck and he pulled her closer to him if that were possible. The kiss was wonderful, and it didn't take her long to learn how the game was played.

She began to return his kisses by plunging her tongue into his mouth and retreating just as he had done.

Roderick's moans told her that he liked what she was doing, and she definitely liked kissing him, but it produced a burning desire in her for something more. A delightful shiver ran through her and robbed her of her strength. He quickly removed her gown and tossed it on the floor. The next kiss was hot and long, and it made her burn to have his hot skin pressing into hers.

Finally, he pulled away from her lips and smiled down at her. Her lips were already swollen. "Ye do that verra well."

She smiled, shyly. "You must be a good teacher."

Roderick lowered his head to trail kisses down her throat while his hand cupped one of her breasts. His thumb stroked her nipple, causing a white-hot fire to surge down her body, and it scared her that she could feel such strong desire. His hand was soon replaced by his mouth as he suckled her nipple. Siena's fingers threaded through his hair and held him to her breast.

He flicked his tongue over her nipple again and again before suckling the other nipple until she was dazed with pleasure and calling his name.

Siena felt so good in his arms. Her instinctive response to him was so powerful. He sensed a passion lay buried deep within her, and he ached to be inside her. It took all the strength that Roderick possessed to draw away from his wife. Every bone in his body was screaming to take her because she belonged to him. She was his wife after all. He waited for his breathing to calm before he spoke.

"That, lass, is lesson number one," he said in a husky voice that sounded strained even to his own ears. He could see her desire in the dim light and was pleased. He flipped her over and pulled her next to him. "Let's get some sleep." He kissed her check and added, "'Tis been a long day. Good night, my love."

"Good night," Siena managed to get out. She realized her gown had been removed and laid in a heap upon the floor. Evidently, she wasn't expected to put it back on because all she could feel was Roderick's hot body pressed intimately against her backside.

She wasn't sure how she felt at the moment. Perhaps a little disappointed. Was that all there was to lovemaking. Maybe she should ask Agatha what she was expected to do. Siena had felt so wonderful a few minutes ago and experienced such emotion that she'd never experienced before. She wanted more. How in the world would she ever go to sleep? Siena didn't have long to wonder because sleep found her. It had been an emotional day and she was exhausted, but as she drifted off to sleep, she had a smile on her face.

Roderick felt disappointed also while he waited patiently for his bride to go to sleep. He'd always taken what he wanted, so where did this consideration come from? Damned if he knew. No red-blooded man should have to be put through such torture without release. He was being noble, he told himself. He shook his head as he eased out of bed and headed for the icy lake. After breaking the ice, the cold water did the trick very quickly and eased his desire.

"Noble hell," he swore to himself.

The woman would be the death of him at this rate.

SIENA TRIED TO STRETCH THE NEXT MORNING, BUT FOUND HER arms were trapped beneath Roderick's arm. She struggled to free herself but in so doing managed to wake him.

"Good morning," she murmured, looking up into his black eyes that were amazingly alert after being woken. "Did you sleep well?"

"Aye. I must have for the sun is up and I've yet to get out of bed."

Siena couldn't believe this man was all hers. She no longer had to fear anyone. Well, she would always fear her father, but he wouldn't ever come to Scotland. "I want to thank you for the flowers you placed in the church," she said, then added, "They were beautiful. I always wanted flowers for my wedding."

"Aye, they were, but it was no my doin' lass, and I've yet to find who did put the roses in the church."

"Strange. I wonder who?" Siena said and questioned if her wish had truly come true because she'd wished it.

"Where anyone found roses in the dead of winter . . . I've no idea, lass, but I'm glad they made ye happy." Roderick pulled her into his arms and kissed her soundly. "Glad to see ye've no forgotten yer lesson," he teased.

Roderick rolled out of bed. He went over and stoked the fire to get the flames going again then he put another log in the grate. Reaching for his clothes, he noticed Siena watching him as he dressed, and he was glad to see she wasn't as shy as last night. Maybe his subtle approach was working.

Siena knew it was rude to stare, but for some reason she couldn't quit watching her husband. He was such a giant of a man, she thought as he slipped a cream-colored linen shirt over his head. She like the tousled appearance of his hair which gave him a rakish look and made her stomach flutter.

Once he had belted his plaid, he tossed the rest of the plaid over his left shoulder. The red color of the plaid made his dark hair stand out. He sat on the bed to pull on his deerskin boots and then he was ready for the day and she hadn't moved an inch.

Suddenly, he turned to her and said, "I will be training this mornin'. After yer breakfast introduce yerself to the kitchen staff. After all, this is yer home now. Ye're in charge." He leaned down and placed a kiss on her forehead and then he was out the door.

Siena needed to pinch herself to prove she wasn't dreaming. Married . . . something she'd never thought would happen to her. She smiled, then stretched her arms overhead. Again, she wondered about the flowers. Could she have made a wish and it simply came true?

Agatha swept into the room, with a big smile upon her face and a tray full of breakfast. "How was last night, milady?"

"D--Different, I think," Siena responded as she slipped out of bed. "Let's sit at the table and eat. I'm starved."

After they sat down, Agatha filled both cups with warm, spiced milk. They each buttered half a bannock before Agatha said, "Well? Are you sore this morning?"

Siena sipped her delicious milk before answering, "We didn't make love last night or I don't think we did. We just kissed."

"What!" Agatha's eyebrows shot up in surprise. "A strong strapping man like that forgo his husbandly rights – why I never."

Siena smiled at the shocked look on Agatha's face. "He is giving me lessons."

"Well, I never."

"I can't believe he is so considerate." Siena sighed. "I sensed there is more, but I was scared last night, and I think he could tell. You know, Roderick isn't anything like his reputation of being merciless.

"So I've seen." Agatha sipped her warm milk. "Indeed, there is more to lovemaking than merely kissing. All women are frightened on their wedding night because they lack experience. "I must say, you don't find many men who are considerate enough to wait."

Siena nodded as she sat her mug down. "I want to ask you about the flowers. Did you put them in the church?"

"Nay, milady. Where would I get flowers? I was a bit surprised myself when I saw them. They were beautiful and filled the church with the best smell."

"Roderick said he didn't know anything about the flowers either. Now I'm left wondering if I did it myself."

"I cannot answer that, milady." Agatha shook her head. "Everyone says that you are gifted . . . maybe you are."

"I don't know if what they say is true, perhaps time will tell. However, I'd love to have some control of these magical things that I do.

"Oh, I forgot to mention to Roderick that I had a vision of his son, Michael when Roderick mixed our blood together in the church. I must remember to tell him. I think the child is alive.

She placed her napkin on the table. "Let's get dressed. I'm supposed to meet the kitchen staff today."

Cook Alva Scott swung a pot over her head, then slammed it down on the counter. She was more than ready to take on the English lass. No one was going to run her kitchen when she'd been doing fine for the last two years.

"I need to set her straight, right away," Alva told Mary, her assistant, who was filling a large cauldron with water. Mary knew better than to express her opinion. Alva was fuming and Mary didn't want something tossed at her head.

Siena appeared in the doorway, almost as if she'd been conjured up. Alva jumped and grabbed her chest. Mary wanted to laugh but didn't.

"I'm sorry. I didn't mean to scare you, but Laird Scott ask me to speak with the head cook," Siena said as she looked at Mary.

"That would be me," Alva said as she dried her hands on a towel.

Siena noticed the belligerent tone of Alva's voice. "I'm Lady Siena and your name is?"

"My name be Alva and I run the kitchens. What do ye need?"

Siena could tell Alva wanted no part of her new mistress. "Actually, I need nothing. My question is what do you need?" Siena almost laughed at the surprised look on the cook's face. At least she had her attention now. "I also would like to see what you have planned for dinner."

"I—I need," Alva stuttered. "I dinna ken, lass."

"Are there any supplies that you need or maybe more help in the kitchen? I'm sure running the kitchen must be difficult feeding so many."

"Aye, milady. I could use one more to help with the preparation of meals and perhaps two more to serve the men at meals."

"Then I shall see that you get someone." Siena smiled. "I'll speak to Laird Scott tonight."

Alva smiled at that bit of news. Perhaps she had misjudged, the wee lass. She told Siena mutton was planned for the dinner tonight. Alva had just finished speaking when the back door suddenly opened blowing in wintery air.

"Alva," a girl with flushed cheeks rushed into the room. "Freddy is feeling poorly. Ye need to come and see him straight away. The Green Lady is busy attending to others and cannot see the child right now."

"Perhaps, I can help," Siena suggested. "I'm a healer, myself."

"Milady would ye do such a thing?"

"I would. Where is the child?"

"He is with the Green Lady," the young girl said.

"I shall go immediately," Siena said, and she rushed out the door.

CHAPTER 12

*B*y the time Siena reached the sickroom, she saw several women sitting around holding either their stomachs or heads, waiting for someone to take care of them. Elen was bent over a patient in the corner. Siena smelled the stuffiness the minute she stepped into the room. "Good day, Elen. How can I help?"

"I'm no so sure 'tis a good day," Elen grumbled as she straightened up, placing her hands on the small of her back when she stretched. "Seems everyone is complaining about a bellyache."

"I'll be happy to help you, but I'd especially like to see Alva's son Freddy. I promised I would take care of him.

"Over there," Elen said with a wave of her pipe.

A small boy with sandy brown hair was curled in a ball on a blanket, clutching his stomach. His eyes were squeezed shut. He reminded Siena of a small puppy with his sad face.

Siena scooped Freddy up in her arms. He moaned as she

placed him on a small cot. "This will feel better than the hard floor," she soothed as she sat on the side of the bed and felt the child's forehead. "Elen, he is burning up. If I had my herbs, I would know what to do for him. Any ideas?"

"My stomach hurts," the child wailed. "My head hurts, too."

"I know little one" Siena brushed the hair off the child's forehead. "We're going to make you feel better soon."

"I'm thinkin' 'tis something they ate, and 'twill have to work its way out of their system if ye ken what I mean." Elen chuckled. "Ye're welcome to use some of my herbs. The bottles are all labeled. Choose what ye will. I've been givin' them barley water for now."

"Do you have any sweet marjoram?" Siena asked. She stood and went to a bowl of cool water so that she could wet a cloth."

"Aye. Found some at the end of last summer. Check the jars."

After Siena placed the cool cloth on Freddy's head, she went over to the shelves and scanned each jar until she found a green jar of marjoram. She opened the lid and smelled the sweet pine scent, then took out a pinch and placed it into a pan of water to heat. Once it had reached the correct temperature, she poured the liquid in a cup, then cooled it by blowing on the water. Next came a dash of honey which she stirred into the cup before giving it to Freddy. After soothing the child, she began taking care of the others until they had seen everyone. Only one woman named Ruby refused Siena's help because the woman saw her birthmark. Ruby threw up her hands in front of her and made the sign of the cross as to ward off evil spirits.

"I'll take care of the old bat," Elen said under her breath. "It appears that yer sweet marjoram has calmed everyone down. I do appreciate yer help, lass."

"I'm still learning my way around, but I'll try and help you more. I promise," Siena said, giving Elen a hug before she left.

Siena was still disturbed that people thought her evil because of her birthmark. She only hoped one day that everyone would think of her as a good person.

LATER THAT NIGHT, SIENA REALIZED SHE WAS VERY TIRED. However, once she took her seat at the high table next to Roderick, her energy returned, and she felt the calmness that Roderick brought to her. A feeling she couldn't explain, but one she liked.

"Have ye had a good day, lass?" Roderick asked, placing a hand on her arm in a tender gesture. "Ye know, lass. I think it's time that ye started wearing my plaid."

"I would have to have someone show me how to wear it."

"That can be arranged. 'Twill keep you warm since even our springs are cool." He rubbed the back of her hand. "Now, tell me about yer day."

Siena's heart fluttered just being this close to her husband, and she wondered how silly she was that his slightest touch could make her feel warm all over and happy.

"We seemed to have a sickness going around, so I helped Elen all afternoon. And before I knew it the day had slipped by."

"You must be tired," Roderick said, but found that his gaze was drawn to Siena's chest and the way her breast strained against the fabric of her gown. He was looking forward to teaching her lesson number two tonight since she had been on his mind most of the day. A thought that both pleased and irritated him at the same time. His mind should be on his men, his clan, and not this slip of a woman.

When she paused, he asked, "Did ye have any problems?"

"A few still don't want any part of me once they see my birthmark. I try to keep my sleeve pulled down, but it slips up as I'm working." She smiled and continued, "However, it's amazing that if you're really sick your opinion can change very fast. I could have horns growing out of my head and they wouldn't care a bit."

Roderick chuckled. "'Twill take time, lass."

"Where are your brothers?"

"They have returned to their holdings. Next week I will go to the Dunham holding to see if I can help with a territorial dispute, but I won't be gone long. There will be enough protection for Black Dawn."

"Do you suppose that one day you'll paint the walls of Black Dawn white again?" Siena asked.

Roderick sighed. "One day when I can put the past completely behind me."

Siena gave him a small smile, hoping that one day the castle would once again be white and their awful past behind them.

They enjoyed the rest of their meal as they drank wine and chatted with others. At the end, Roderick leaned over and whispered, "Go upstairs, lass. Take off all yer clothes and wait under the covers for me. Tonight, is lesson number two."

Siena cheeks burned at his words. She nodded and excused herself from the table, heading for their room.

Thankfully, Agatha was busy talking to Duncan and didn't notice Siena's red cheeks when she told Agatha to stay behind, that she would be fine.

SIENA WASN'T QUITE SURE HOW SHE FELT AS SHE LAY NAKED under the covers, remembering the night before and how wonderful the kisses had been. She had a burning desire for another kiss. Heat rippled under her skin in anticipation, wondering what tonight would be like.

The door swung open and in the soft glow of the firelight she watched Roderick stroll over to one of the chairs where he sat down to remove his brown boots. He didn't say anything as he slipped his shirt over his head, tossing it on the nearby chair, his gaze never leaving hers. Next, he unbuckled his belt, letting his kilt fall around his feet. She could see all his muscular body at one time as he strolled toward the bed, but she didn't look away this time and she did remember to breathe.

Her husband was magnificent.

Roderick slipped beneath the covers and gathered her in his arms. The next thing she knew he was leaning over her, placing feathery kisses on her face. Siena sighed. Her arms slipped around him, and she pressed her body into his, causing a low growl to issue from Roderick. That pleased her.

"I see you remember lesson one verra wull, lass."

"Aye," she replied breathlessly. "I'm a fast learner."

He kissed her ear, tugging on one of her earlobes, and then he moved lower as he continued to explore her soft flesh, placing light kisses on her neck. She went limp as shivers of desire ran through her.

Raising his mouth for a moment, he gazed into her eyes and saw her desire as he lowered his head to kiss her. His tongue touched her lips, urging them to part and the minute that she did he plunged his tongue into her mouth, mating with hers.

She was fully aware of the hardness of his thighs pressed next to her as his fingers stroked the back of her neck. This kiss was different and more demanding as if he were telling her he wanted more. She began to play with his tongue and was shocked at her own eager response. Her blood felt like it was on fire. His magnificent kisses were driving her crazy.

Roderick felt Siena moving restless against him. He had to admit that she had learned her first lesson well, and he was surprised how his body burned for her. A strange feeling that he couldn't remember ever feeling before. He'd had sex in the year since his wife's death, but it was just that, sex. This was different. A growl of satisfaction slipped from his lips. Then he reminded himself he needed to go slow. After all, this was her first time. He would teach her the second lesson and then on the third lesson she would be his. He trailed kisses down to her swollen breast where he took one of the red tipped buds into his mouth. He began to suckle, pulling and tugging until he heard her gasps of pleasure.

He lifted his head and smiled at her as he said, "Lesson number two."

And then he was kissing her again and again until she couldn't think straight. Passion rose in her like the hottest fire. She thought she would explode. The way he held her betrayed his hunger and she opened her mouth further. She needed to taste all of him. How in the world would she survive a third lesson? There had to be more. And she wanted it all. And that is when she moaned a single word, "Please."

Roderick heard her. Blood pounded in his brain. His senses sizzled as her body sprang to life. There would be no other lessons. His wife was driving him crazy. He couldn't remember wanting anyone as much as he wanted Siena. As he reached down and stroked her soft curls, she bucked against his hand and he felt her wetness. She was ready for him. He spread her thighs with his knee then slipped his hands beneath her hips to lift her up to receive him. Slowly, he slipped in and then withdrew. He needed to go slow but the blood pounding in his head pushed him on to feel her silken warm. He drove fully into her and stopped; his breathing ragged.

She tensed and cried out.

"Are you…" he gasped.

"I—I," Siena trailed off as she moved her hips, wondering what was missing. She had felt a sharp pain, but it seemed to be easing. Surely this mating wasn't to be painful. He began to move again slowly at first and then she could feel a pressure replacing the pain, and she wanted to shout thank God. Roderick moved faster and faster, plunging and withdrawing until Siena felt herself being washed away in a sea of desire as Roderick drove into her once last time. They soared with the intense pleasure exploding in their bodies until the peak of delight washed over both of them.

Roderick wanted to say something as he lay on top of her trying to catch his breath. He braced his arms so that he wouldn't crush her.

He heard her whisper, "I--I don't think I can stand a third lesson."

Roderick chuckled, then rolled to his side and pulled his wife next to him, keeping her cradled in his arms. He was truly a satisfied man and he was happy for the first time in a long, long while.

"I think yer lessons are complete, lass." He drew in another breath and said in a ragged voice, "Ye're mine lass, completely."

When Siena didn't respond, he tilted his head down to look at her and found she was fast asleep.

Roderick wasn't too sure if that was a good thing or a bad thing. At least she had a smile on her face.

CHAPTER 13

The next few months were the happiest that Siena could ever remember. She had brought color to the great hall with the many banners that she'd had hung on the walls. Now it didn't look so drab and dull. She also kept busy helping the sick or those who would let her. Some were still very standoffish; however, she felt like she was making a difference.

Her husband was very loving at night, but he still had that haunted look in his eyes that she wished she could erase. She knew Michael was the reason, but so far, she couldn't see anything about the child, making her doubt that she did have a special gift. She wanted to tell Roderick about seeing Michael in her vision at the church, but she still wasn't sure of her abilities yet. She prayed that this would change. She definitely didn't want to get Roderick's hope up until she could tell him something firm.

The days had turned warmer or should she say the snow

had melted and now it was cool but not freezing. Elen sent word to Siena that she needed to gather herbs and she'd like for Siena to go with her. Siena dressed in her *arisaid,* having learned how to wear the plaid, she'd gotten good about wearing it around her shoulders and tied at the waist with a belt to keep warm. However, she still wore her underskirt that she'd had a pouch sewn into the fabric for her precious stores.

Siena was more than ready to get outside now that the weather was nicer, and Agatha said she wanted to go along also. It seemed that everyone was ready for fresh air and sunshine.

They waited outside for Elen to join them, and together they made their way to the stables.

Garvin brought out the horses. "Do ye have the laird's permission, I might ask?"

Siena looked at him with a puzzled expression. "Should we?"

"Aye, ye should. He is training down in the lower bailey. Be sure to stop by before ye leave so he dinna take off the top of me head."

"Quit ye fussing and help me up," Elen instructed.

"Can ye handle the horse?"

"I ain't dead, lad," Elen said.

Agatha laughed and so did Siena as they left with Garvin's mouth hanging wide open.

Elen led the way down to the lower bailey, where Roderick was practicing with swords. It appeared he was training the younger soldiers.

He disarmed his opponent as they rode up, then he swung around so fast it startled Siena. She gasped. She could see the strength of a warrior in him. He jabbed the tip of his sword in the ground when he saw them. "Where are ye goin'?"

"We need to gather herbs," Siena said.

"Ah, wull, I need to send someone with ye, and you still dinna answer my question as to where." But before they could answer his question, he turned to Elen. "Are ye able to ride, Elen?"

"I'm hundred and three, lad and was sitting a saddle before ye could walk."

Roderick smiled and held his hands up in defense. "I've no doubt, but do ye have a way of protecting yerselves? And where are ye goin'?"

Elen rolled her eyes before answering, "We're going to the glen where the blue *burn* is located to see if the hawthorn tree is blooming."

Siena was glad that Elen answered because she hadn't bothered to ask where they were going. She was just glad to be outside and riding. "I have my bow and arrows," Siena answered his other question. "I can protect us."

She saw Roderick look at the bow she had slung around her body. "But can ye hit anything, lass?"

Siena took offense to Roderick assuming that she couldn't hit her target or do anything because she was a woman, so she snapped her answer, "I believe I can."

He didn't appear to believe her as he stood hands on hips not saying a word. "There is a target on that tree." He pointed to the end of the field. "Let me see you hit the center."

"Would you like me to shoot from my horse or on the ground?"

He didn't answer her barb, but he was gentleman enough to help her down from her mount.

"Show me the target again," Siena said as she pulled her bow over her head.

Roderick took the bow from her and one of her arrows. "I'll

show ye." He pulled the string tight and let his arrow fly hitting the dummy right where a heart should be."

He smugly handed the bow back to her. "'Tis easy."

Siena definitely wanted to wipe the smirk off his face. Slowly, she pulled the string straight back, the arrow even with her mouth and let the arrow fly.

It hit in one of the painted eyes.

She wanted to laugh at his dumbfounded expression but thought it wise not to. "Aye, it was easy," she said, then added, "I figured an eye was just as good as the heart. Either way, the man will not be going anywhere."

The men who stood around them cheered as she went back to her mount where Roderick graciously helped her back up.

"The lass has proven herself," he said with a smile.

Elen cleared her throat and asked, "If the hawthorn is blooming ye ken what it means?"

"Aye, I do. *Beltane*."

Siena had no idea what they were talking about, but she was ready to go for a ride. "You can always come with us," Siena said to Roderick, wanting to have him for company.

"I've training, lass," he replied. "Now be off with ye, but dinna go any further."

After promising, they left the castle before Roderick could change his mind. Siena felt like he was treating all of them like children. What could a ride in the hills hurt? Then she thought about *Beltane* and rode up beside Elen to ask her, "What is *Beltane*?"

Elen removed her pipe. "When the hawthorn tree blooms, 'tis a signal of the beginnin' of summer, lass, and that is when we have the *Beltane* feast to celebrate summer. My bones will surely welcome the warmer air."

"Did you say that we will have a feast?" Agatha asked.

"Aye. 'Twill be verra special. There will be big bonfires lit on the hilltops, and all the hearth fires are extinguished to be rekindled with the cherished flames from the bonfires."

They were winding their way down a single path to a small *burn* so they couldn't talk. The stream was beautiful with crystal clear water flowing over rocks that sent water in many different directions.

"That sounds like a nice ritual," Siena said. "In England, they dance around a Maypole, so I've been told as I've never seen it before."

"I saw it once in my younger days," Agatha said, then added. "It was pretty with different colored ribbons."

Siena dismounted once they reached the water's edge and so did Agatha. They turned to look at Elen who hadn't budged. Siena wondered if Elen needed help.

Elen smiled. "I said I could ride, but gettin' on and off this beast is entirely different, so I'll stay seated if ye dinna mind." She pointed her pipe. "There is our hawthorn tree."

"Look it has flowers!" Siena exclaimed.

"Pick the flowers and put in one bag and the leaves in another. In the fall there will be berries so we will come back and get those, too."

It was a glorious day without a single cloud in the sky as Siena and Agatha picked the precious flowers. The blooms came in clusters of white flowers with red dots on the petals.

Siena clipped the last of the clusters and slipped it into a bag. She had left a lot of blooms because she didn't see any need of stripping the tree when they had what they needed. "This is more like a bush than a tree."

"Aye," Elen said as she puffed on her pipe. "This is a young tree, but it will grow bigger. Be sure to get some of the tender leaves."

"They make a good tincture for sore throats," Siena explained to Agatha who knew nothing about medicine.

"I believe I could use some now," Agatha grumbled. "My throat has been a little sore."

"We'll have to take care of that once we return," Siena said. She pointed. "I see some heather which is good for the kidneys, coughs and colds. I must have some of that as it will not be in full bloom until late summer."

"'Tis unusual, lass that it is blooming now, but lucky for us."

Siena hurried over to the one purple bush and she caught the light floral scent which she liked. She reached into the bush and picked several of the sprigs. In the middle of the purple she spotted two sprigs of white heather, something she'd never seen before. She reached to snip the white buds. The minute she touched the white sprigs she caught a glimpse of Michael. He was crying and asking when he was going to go home to his father. She gasped and clutched her breast.

"What is wrong, lass?" Elen asked.

Siena turned toward her. "I just caught a glimpse of Michael and he is alive, but I don't know where he is located."

"'Twas the white heather," Elen said. "'Tis known to be lucky."

Just then something swept by Siena and she screamed and jumped. She wasn't sure what it was, but it was big. She moved as fast as she could back to where she'd left her bow, but she wasn't fast enough as something caught her skirt and she heard the material rip.

Elen's horse reared and the other two horses scattered.

"Go for help!" Siena screamed just as she reached her bow.

She jerked it up and positioned her bow just as the animal swung around to come at her again. She took deadly aim, knowing that if she missed the animal would defiantly hit her and most likely kill her with his tusk. The animal's black eyes were wild and his tusks long as he barreled down upon her. The arrow was swift. It caught the animal in the eye. With a squeal he fell to the ground and slid to her feet.

Siena's knees were shaking so bad she could hardly stand, but then she heard Agatha scream, "T--there is another one, milady!" She ran right past Siena with the boar chasing right behind her. Again, Siena's aim was true as she caught the animal between the eyes.

Siena was shaking so bad that her teeth were chattering. "I—I do believe that I need to sit down." She staggered over to a smooth rock. She didn't realize that tears were streaming down her cheeks, but when she let go of her bow, she realized that she still held the white sprig of white heather in her hand.

Everything would be all right.

CHAPTER 14

The sound of thunder rumbled in the distance.

The ground shook.

Siena looked up. There wasn't a cloud in the sky. Surely there could be no more boars because she didn't have the strength to move. She could hear Agatha screaming and crying in the background.

As the rumble grew closer, Siena turned to her left and saw Roderick and his men galloping toward her. Before she could blink, he jerked Hercules to a halt and was on his feet running toward her, his sword drawn ready for battle.

"What the hell!" Roderick bellowed as he noticed the dead boars at Siena's feet. His heart was beating so fast that he had to pause before he could speak again. In the short time that it had taken him to get to her, he realized that he could never lose Siena because he had an overwhelming need to protect her, but there was something more. She meant more to him than he ever thought possible.

He knelt down beside her and took her trembling hand in his. "Are ye injured, lass?"

"Saints above!" Duncan shouted from behind Roderick. "Och, the lass has taken down two boars. How in the hell did the lass do that?"

"They dinna hurt ye?" Roderick asked again as he checked Siena's body for injuries.

"N--No, they just scared me," Siena finally admitted as she dashed the tears from her face. She was shaking so bad that her voice trembled. "T—They came out of nowhere. I—I barely had time to shoot them." She couldn't believe Roderick was here. She desperately needed his comfort. As if he read her thoughts, he pulled her to him and wrapped his arms around her, then rested his chin on the top of her head.

"And that was one of the reasons I dinna like ye ridin' without a guard. Ye scairt the hell out of me, lass." He took a deep breath. "Elen sounded like a banshee when she met us screaming for help and waving her pipe in the air."

Siena brought her hand up to stifle her giggles as she pictured what Elen must have looked like riding disheveled on her horse. "Now I can see that a guard would have been good, however, I also was capable of protecting myself," she pointed out.

Roderick felt that Siena was gaining control of herself again because she'd stopped trembling and he hated to admit that what she said was true. The lass seemed most capable. "Aye, but ye still could have been hurt and I would no forgive myself if you were hurt. `Twas a good thing that I'd ridden out to see how ye were faring when I met Elen."

Siena pushed back from him, then changed the subject. "We

got our herbs so I guess we can go back to the keep," she said as she stood back.

"Aye. And now we can have roasted boar for the feast tonight. Everyone will be happy about that," Roderick said, then looked at his men. "We'll need to get these animals back to the keep and get them dressed for tonight's feast. Tonight, we celebrate *Beltane.*"

"I don't see, Star," Siena said as she looked around. "She must have bolted during all the commotion."

"Aye," Roderick said. "'Tis one of the things that caught my attention. Yers and Agatha's horses coming back without riders was not a good sign. Star was a silver blur as she raced back to the keep. Come on, ye can ride with me." He helped her up on Hercules' broad back.

"Duncan, are ye goin' to take Agatha back?"

"Aye. Just as soon as she quits shaking." Duncan chuckled. He had his arm around Agatha waist. "No sure the lass can walk just yet."

"It isn't funny," Agatha grumbled. "We both could have been dead if it were not for milady's skills."

"I agree with that," Duncan said as he shoved Agatha up on his horse then mounted behind her. "Laird, ye best not challenge yer lady to a shootin' match. No sure ye would win."

"Oh, aye, I think ye could be correct, Duncan." Roderick pulled Siena back against him. "She might best me with the bow and arrows." *But she was still a woman,* he thought and *needed* his protection.

As the sun lowered in the sky, the lower bailey began to come alive as the clan members gathered in groups laughing and drinking as they waited for the pigs to be done.

The children were kicking a ball and chasing after it. Giggling filled the air, making everyone smile.

With the lighthearted mood, she didn't feel like an outsider tonight. People were not turning away from her as they once had when she first arrived. The men were all talking in groups, laughing and slapping each other on the back. Kegs of whisky had been carried outside so that everyone could drink and enjoy themselves.

The roasting boars smelled wonderful as she walked beside Roderick who paused to talk to a few of his men. The soldiers raised cups of ale to her for providing the meat.

Fergus was grinning from ear to ear. He brushed the ale off his red beard and held his cup up. "I think the lass needs one more toast. To the lass who has bested all of us in huntin', probably why the laird married her, so we'd always have food on the table.

Siena bowed her head. "Thank you, Fergus for the high praise. I assure you I was merely lucky today."

Siena held Roderick's hand as they moved down the path. "It is a good thing we went real early this morning for the herbs, so they had time to roast the pig."

"Aye. We also split the boar down the middle so it will cook faster and with our days growing longer that has also helped the feast."

They stopped at a place on the hill and spread their blankets where others had done the same. There was a huge tree blocking them from the others, so it offered a little privacy. "Is this a good place?" she asked.

"Aye," Roderick said. He sat down leaning against the thick tree trunk, and then he pulled Siena in front of him so she could lean back against him. "Watch the hill." He pointed. "'Tis time for the fires."

The hill in the distance could be seen clearly in the setting sun. Suddenly, two large fires burst orange and red until the flames were leaping high in the air. She gasped. She wasn't sure what she had expected, but it sure wasn't such a big fire. The clan members cheered. She wondered what the fires meant.

"I hear cows," Siena said. And sure, enough in the distance, she saw the herd marching up the hill single file.

"Aye. 'Tis time to lead the herd to summer pastures, but before they can be led into the field there has to be a rite of purification."

"I don't understand."

"The coos will walk between the two fires." He pointed at the hill. "I should say they will be herded between the two fires because they would no go willingly."

She loved to hear his accent when he said cows, but she still didn't understand. "Why? Isn't it dangerous for the animals?"

"Dinna worry, lass. There is plenty of room for the animals. The white coos will walk between the two fires and 'twill singe their fur turning them brown. Therefore, it will signal they have moved from winter to summer."

Siena started laughing. "You made that up."

"Nay, I've seen it done many times since I was a wee bairn. We've many rituals and superstitions here."

"I believe you." She turned so that she could see him. He propped up a leg so she could lean against it and face him while they talked. "And things I never have thought possible do happen." She reached into her pouch and pulled out the small piece of white heather.

"Ah, wull. Here's proof. 'Tis said to be verra lucky that if ye take white heather into battle then ye'll no lose yer fight."

"Well, when I picked the sprig," she paused and gathered her courage before she continued, "I heard Michael ask when he was going to see his father." She grabbed Roderick's arms. "I believe Michael is alive, but I don't know where he is."

For a few minutes, Roderick didn't say anything. He appeared stunned. And this from a man who never showed any emotion. "Ah, lass. I want it to be true and can only hope that ye'll find my son."

Since they were secluded by the big tree. Roderick enfolded Siena in his arms and gently kissed her. Then he deepened the kiss and kissed her hungrily. His tongue coaxing her lips open so he could taste all of her sweetness. His tongue stroked and mated with hers until he felt her tremble in his arms. It took all of his willpower to not go any further.

For a long moment she felt as if she were floating. The kiss was exhilarating, but they were at a celebration, so she pulled back. "Keep the heather until we find Michael."

After the bonfire merry making they made their way back to the keep, they smiled at each other. "I think everyone is enjoying *Beltane*."

"Aye, they are. 'Tis always nice to have winter behind us and you made it special, lass, with the two boars. They have never had that much meat at one time."

Alva waved at her with her son by her side. The rest of the kitchen staff was outside also, but so far, she had not seen Elen and she wondered where she could be.

Siena spotted Agatha who was laughing with Duncan. Siena

had never seen her look so young. "Have you notice that Duncan and Agatha seemed to get along very well?"

"Aye, I think that Duncan likes Agatha very much." Roderick laughed. "Could have another wedding coming up, lass."

"I hope so. Agatha deserves to be happy."

The air was filled with the aroma of roast boar. A pit with two spits were set up in the middle of the crowd. All the women had fixed side dishes and they were lined up along the tables.

When it was time and the cooks had declared the pig was done a cheer went up and everyone filed by the boars with their trenchers to get a big portion of pig.

Roderick insisted that he and Siena would go last to honor his clan.

He was a good one, Siena thought.

Just as they were getting ready to get their food, Elen marched across the compound dressed in all her glorious green color. Roderick was speaking with Duncan and not paying them any attention.

"You are defiantly The Green Woman tonight." Siena laughed.

"Have to hold up my reputation, lass. I should have known that ye could take care of yerself. How do ye like our *Beltane?*"

"I think it is a very nice celebration. Still cannot believe the cows change from white to brown, however."

"Ye of all people should believe." Elen laughed. "I've been busy putting out all the fires in the keep. Tonight, after ye have eaten, you and the laird will go to the bonfire and pick up a stick to light the fire in your room. 'Tis considered lucky."

"Aye, we will," Siena said.

Then Elen leaned in to whisper, "*Beltane* is the union of

Earth and Sky. Tonight, ye will be sensual and passionate with the joy of conception."

Siena jerked back and she felt her face burn as Elen laughed and went on her merry way. Lovemaking wasn't something Siena cared to talk about to anyone but Roderick. Now she wondered if tonight she would conceive.

She guessed time would tell.

CHAPTER 15

Balan Castle
    Northumbria, England

$\mathcal{B}$alan Castle stands on a somewhat elliptical mound overlooking the River Wansbeck. Flags flew from the towers. By all appearances, everything looked peaceful, but turmoil was brewing inside the castle's gray walls.

Baron Cinge Bertram sat behind his desk drumming his fingers upon the desk. His outlook was dire. He admitted to himself that he'd been a spendthrift and squandered much of his wealth, but he had always had Berwick and his son's men to back him up . . . until that damn Scot took Berwick and killed his son.

Now that his son had been gone for over a year. He didn't have enough men to retake Berwick and guard his own castle.

He'd love to attack Black Dawn as his son once had and hopefully murder Laird Scott.

But Cinge knew he couldn't do that. His only pleasure was knowing that the laird suffered every day for the loss of his son.

A knock on the door interrupted his brooding thoughts. "Enter."

"Sire, Lord Malcolm is here to see you."

"Show him in," Cinge barked. He straightened his jacket, so he'd look presentable instead of desperate. He ran his hands through his brown hair, slicking it back away from his face.

In no time, Lord Malcolm strolled into the library and Cinge motioned for the man to take a seat. Malcolm reminded Cinge of a fat rat with his beady eyes. "Would you care for something to drink?"

"I'll have what you are drinking."

Cinge poured another glass of red port into a goblet and refilled his own, then sat the bottle on his desk. When he handed Malcolm his glass, Cinge asked, "What can I do for you?"

"It's what I can do for you." Lord Malcolm laughed at the shocked look on Cinge's face.

"I beg your pardon?"

"I know you lost Berwick Castle along with a sizable income," Malcolm said each word with the certainty of a man who was determined to get what he wanted. "I'm here to offer you a deal."

"Go on."

With a casual nod, Malcolm said, "I want your daughter."

Cinge tried to hide his surprise at Malcolm's request. Cinge blinked several times before he said, "My daughter has been a thorn in my side for years. Why would you want her?"

Malcolm laughed. "Well for one, I hear she has grown into a beautiful woman. I've also been told that she can lead me to the Holy Grail."

"The Holy Grail has been lost for years, man. There have been many quests for the Grail . . . all ending in death."

"Death, maybe." Malcolm shrugged. "Yet none have found the cup. Once it's in my possession then I can make you a very wealthy man."

Cinge nodded. "I like what I'm hearing but Siena is with Laird Scott, so I will have to get her back on English soil."

Malcolm leaned forward and placed his glass on the desk. He refilled his glass, then asked, "Do you have the men to take her from the laird?"

"Hell no!" Cinge shrugged matter-of-factly and then thought better, not wanting to show his weakness. "Well, not on his ground, but I do have something the man wants more than anything. I think Laird Scott will hand over my daughter without lifting a sword."

Malcolm astonishment was obvious, but he recovered and asked, "Then we have a bargain?"

Cinge stood and raised his glass in salute to Lord Malcolm. "We have a deal. I'll send a message right away."

———

ONE SPRING MORNING, RODERICK TOLD SIENA HE WAS GOING ON a raid with two of his brothers. She bade him to be careful and vowed to herself that she was going to find Michael while her husband was gone. As she watched Roderick ride away, she had the strangest feeling that she'd never see him again. She shook her head to get rid of the silly feeling. He wouldn't be gone that long. He had said so himself. She would make her husband happy again as soon as she discovered where Michael was located.

Two days later, Siena returned to the keep from her morning walk, she found a messenger standing in the entryway with the steward standing in front of him with his arms crossed. Martin, Roderick's steward, more or less ran the household and had been very nice to Siena since she'd arrived. She assumed the men were having a discussion, so she made her way down the hall leading to the stairs that led to the great hall, knowing she wasn't needed.

Martin turned and said, "Milady, the mon says he has a message for Laird Scott."

Siena paused and then went back to stand next to Martin. "I'm Laird Scott's wife. I'll take it." Siena held out her hand.

"Ye can read, milady?" Martin asked, a surprised look on his face as most women and men he knew couldn't read and he most certainly couldn't.

"Aye, I can."

The messenger, who she noticed was dressed in her father's colors, handed her the small note. She immediately recognized her father's seal; however, she didn't bother to comment or show any outer expression as a chill ran up her back. She knew that this couldn't be good.

"Is there a reply, milady?" the messenger asked.

"Tell him, Laird Scott will be back in a couple of days. He will send his reply then," Siena managed to say in a strained voice.

Her feet felt like lead as she went down the stairs into the great hall. Once she was alone, she walked over to one of the chairs by the fireplace and sat down. Siena realized she was shaking from head to toe so she took several deep breaths to calm herself before opening the letter. Quickly, she scanned the hateful words.

Agatha strolled in from the kitchen with two cups of hot spiced milk and sat them on the table between the two chairs. "I thought you might like something warm this morning, milady," she paused and peered at Siena. "What's wrong? You look like you have seen a ghost."

"I wish I had seen a ghost." Siena held up the slip of paper. "This is a letter from my father who I assure you is very much alive."

Agatha gasped and set her cup back down before she dropped it. "What does it say?"

"Father has Michael."

"That's wonderful. The laird's son is not dead. Laird Scott will be so happy."

"Yes, that part is great news. However, Michael is still in the hands of my father. I hope he hasn't mistreated the child, but I fear he probably has." Siena paused and took a sip of milk, her mind spinning. "He wants Roderick to make a trade . . . his son for me."

"Laird Scott will never agree."

"How could he not make the trade?" Siena asked. "He wants his son more than anything and I want Michael back with his father. Nothing in the world would make Roderick happier."

"But the laird loves you, milady, I'm sure he will think of something. He would never make the trade." Agatha frowned. "I don't like that look in your eye, milady. What are you going to do?"

"I don't know. I'm going to sit here a few minutes and think," Siena said as she stared into the fire wanting the fire to speak to her. Then she remembered the stones. She slipped her right hand into her pouch and slipped the four stones into her hand. She held them tightly in her hand and murmured, "Speak to me. Show me the boy."

In the middle of the flames, she could see the child. He was in her old bedroom. Michael was very thin, pale, and crying. Her heart ached for the child. He looked so frightened. She definitely knew how that felt. Then the flames produced her father's face and she jumped back bumping the back of her head on the chair. He was talking to Henry, his first in command.

"WE WILL LOOK LIKE WE ARE GOING TO MAKE THE EXCHANGE, BUT once the boy is almost to his father you will shoot an arrow into the boy's back and kill him. Let Roderick feel what is like to truly lose a son. I'll have no more use for the boy.

"What about your daughter?" Henry asked.

A slow smile spread on her father's face. "I do have use for her."

SIENA WAS BREATHING HARD WHEN SHE JERKED BACK TO THE present. She peered at Agatha who was sitting on the edge of her chair. "It's a trap."

"What did you see?"

"My father is planning to kill the boy in front of Roderick to even the score for my brother's death."

Agatha gasped. "But you did the killing, milady."

"Aye, but I'm not sure he knows that I killed my brother, however, my father needs me, so he cannot kill me. Of that I am sure."

"Milady, we must do something."

"Do you remember that there is a passage in the back of the castle?" It was built because my father didn't want to see servants running around the castle."

"Aye."

"I think I can get into the castle and get the child out without anyone seeing me."

Agatha shook her head, then gasped. "It is awfully danger-ous, milady."

"I don't want Roderick doing battle with my father's men. I don't want to be the cause of men losing their lives when I can make a difference. I can get Michael and we can head back toward Black Dawn."

"But they will notice the child is gone and come after you."

Siena looked around the room as if she was trying to find the answer. "I know." She swung back. "The kitchen staff has always been loyal to me. I will get some food from them and ask that they keep up the pretense that the boy is still in his room for a little while. Father wouldn't bother to check on the boy every day. That will give us a little time. Before I leave, I'll dispatch a messenger to Roderick telling him what is going on. With luck, he will meet us on the road home, and no one will get caught."

"But what if *you* are caught?"

Siena frowned. "I'll tell them that if they let the boy go then I will lead them to the Holy Grail. They have been looking for it for years."

"You know where it is?"

"Not exactly." Siena stood up with a half-smile. "But I have confidence now that I can find it.

"I need to go see the fairies."

CHAPTER 16

*A*fter explaining to Agatha that she could not go with her, Siena grabbed her cloak and hurried to the kitchen where Alva stopped her to approve the dinner menu. Siena nodded, knowing she wouldn't be there to enjoy the meal. She didn't want the household to know she was leaving Black Dawn. She sighed, then she hurried out the back door.

Siena knew she had the strength to rescue the child. She would not fail. Across the lawn, she saw a puff of smoke drifting up in the air and knew that Elen, too, was visiting the fairies.

"Hello," Siena said, once she reached them.

Elen jumped, startled. "Oh, lass," she said, grabbing her chest. "Ye gave me a fright."

Siena saw Elen's face was bright red, so Siena asked, "Are you feeling poorly?"

"Something isn't right, lass," Elen said, shaking her head.

"I've no felt like this since we were attacked, and then I dinna move fast enough to warn everyone."

Barra fluttered in front of Elen, bobbing up and down. "Aye, Elen is correct and I bet you can tell us what is wrong, Siena."

"Actually, I can," Siena replied. "I've come to ask for your help, Barra."

"Help?" Elen grabbed Siena's arm. "What are ye talkin' about, lass?"

"M--Michael is alive!" A sense of power came to Siena and she rushed on, "My father is holding him at the castle where I grew up."

"How do you know this?" Barra asked.

"A note came for Roderick today. Since he isn't here, I opened the message. It said that my father wants to exchange the boy for me," Siena paused, "but he lied. He will kill Michael for revenge for my brother's death."

"So, this is why my head hurts," Elen said. "When something affects the clan like this, then I always get these terrible headaches." She took a couple of puffs from her pipe. "Dinna fear, our laird will know what to do."

"No!" Siena shouted. They both looked at her. "I don't want anyone to lose their life over me."

"But Laird Scott will no want ye in danger," Elen argued.

"It's better to lose me than to lose his son. Besides, if my plan works, we both will escape and no one will die," she spoke with firmness, then she peered at Barra. "I need to able to use my magic if I'm going to rescue Michael, and I'll need your help."

Barra fluttered up and down. "How may I help you?"

"You have given me the stones which are how I know what my father is planning. But can I go and get Michael and bring him back here?" Siena held her hand out and Barra landed on her palm.

"You have always had the power to go where you want to."

"But how?"

"All you have to do is think hard about the place where you want to be, close your eyes and you will be there."

"But what about coming back?"

"You can come back, but you cannot bring someone else with you."

"That won't work. I need to get Michael back safely." Siena thought for a moment. "I know. The castle has many back hallways and passages. I'll go and get Michael and then escape out the back of the castle, but we will need horses."

Barra giggled. "I can help you there. I'll come with you, as I don't count as someone else," she giggled again. "I have my own powers so I can get the horses you need to return. I'll also stay with you for a little extra magic."

"I would hug you," Siena said. "If I were not afraid of damaging your wings."

"That's all right," Barra said with a magical laugh. "I'm glad to help."

"Are ye both crazy?" Elen said, jerking her arms straight up in the air. "Ye will be in the enemy camp with many men. Ye should wait for our laird." Elen shook her head. "He will no be pleased."

"Roderick will forget about his anger once he sees his son." Siena clenched her jaw to kill the sob in her throat. "And I'll be accomplishing his greatest wish . . . to have his son home safe and sound."

"I'm one hundred and ten, lass. Ye should listen to me. He'll no be happy if ye are killed in the process."

Siena hugged Elen, wondering if Elen truly knew her own age. "Thank you for caring, Elen. I'll send word to Roderick as soon as I leave so that he might meet us on the way home. Everything will work out. Wait and see."

"Ye have powerful magic," Elen paused, then continued, "it will take everything ye have to accomplish this task."

"I know," Siena replied.

Siena hurried back to the castle to talk to Agatha. She explained to Agatha what she was going to do and persuaded her to switch cloaks as Agatha's was a dark color and would draw less notice.

Siena ran upstairs to retrieve Michael's rabbit and then rushed back down.

After assuring Agatha that she would be all right, Siena instructed her to send word to Roderick and tell him what has happened, then she went back to the fairy mound and waited for Barra.

"Are you ready?" Barra asked, in her little girl's voice. The other fairies fluttered around like flies, wishing them well.

"I am," Siena replied. Barra flew over and sat on Siena's shoulder. Siena spun around three times. Everything grew black as the air rushed past them and then they were sucked into nothing . . . no sight . . . no sound . . . no feeling.

THEY LANDED BEHIND HER FATHER'S CASTLE AT THE EDGE OF THE woods. Siena felt like a feather floating through the air. It would have been the perfect way to escape with Michael, however, Barra had explained that you had to be magical to fly from one place to another and the child wasn't magical.

The gray walls of Balan Castle loomed ahead of them, and luckily the soldiers were not patrolling the back wall. The small door couldn't be seen unless you knew where it was located, so Siena didn't expect any problems.

She looked at Barra, "Will someone see you?"

"Nay. Only children and *special* people can see fairies. I'll go and get two horses and wait for you here in the woods just in case there is a patrol."

Siena nodded.

"And do be careful, Siena, as they *can* see you."

Siena smiled. *It felt good to have someone worry about her*, she thought as she turned and headed toward the wall. Once there, she ran her hand across the cold stone until she felt the small knot in the wall. She pressed the knot and the door popped loose. With her fingertips, she pried the door open, leaving it cracked so she could see in the dark tunnel. She entered and reached for the torch and the flints, but the flints were not there. She wondered who had moved them and prayed that maybe she didn't remember correctly, surely no one knew about this passageway.

Siena clutched her stones, took a deep breath, and blew on the end of the torch and it glowed brightly with orange and yellow flames. Her magic had served her well today. Perhaps she was getting better using her gift. She lit the other torch and left it in the bracket by the outer door, then she closed the door, leaving the outside world behind her.

Carefully, she walked down the stone passageway, ducking spider webs. It was cool and dark. Her breath sounded loud in her ears as she went deeper and deeper in the passageway until she reached the stairs. All her senses were strained, expecting every minute to be discovered. She started to climb the two flights of stairs until she came to the end which opened behind a chest in her old bedroom. She placed the torch in a bracket so they could use it on the way out, then she listened at the door to see if anyone was in her old room.

Nothing.

Slowly she inched the door open, so as not to scare the child. "Michael, pull the chest away from the door." Luckily the child did as he was told. When she had the door open enough to get in, she slipped into the room, and immediately put her finger over her lips so Michael wouldn't scream. His eyes were as big as saucers, but thankfully he remained quiet.

Siena knelt down so she'd be at eye level with the child. "Do you remember me, Michael?"

The child nodded. He jumped into her arms. "I want to go home. That mean man said my da didn't want me anymore."

"Such nonsense. Your father has been worried sick about you." She hugged the child tight, trying to reassure him. "I have something for you." She pulled out his rabbit and handed it to Michael. He latched on to it as if it would protect him from anything.

"I'm here to take you home," Siena said as she rocked the child back and forth. "But you will have to be very quiet and brave because we don't want to get caught. If my father comes in before I can get you out, then you must pretend I'm not here. Do you understand?"

Michael pulled back. "He is your da?"

"Unfortunately, he is but he doesn't love me as your father loves you."

A spark of hope entered the child's eyes. "Is my da here?"

"He is not but he will meet us on the way home." She prayed that what she said was true and Roderick was on his way. "He'll be so excited to see you. He had no idea where you were all this time, and he feared you were dead."

Michael smiled. Siena thought it probably had been a long time since the child had done so. Now there was hope in his eyes instead of sadness.

"I want you to sit on the bed with your rabbit. I'll be right back. I'm going to the kitchen to get some food for our journey home." She noticed Michael was dressed in a nightshirt. "Put your clothes on so you will be ready to go when I come back from the kitchen but stay under the cover in case someone opens the door to check on you."

Siena hurried down the corridor, then down the back steps to the kitchen. Peering around the corner, she spotted Elsa, the gray-haired cook, by herself.

"Elsa," Siena called in a soft voice. "I need your help."

"I don't believe my eyes." Elsa ran over and grasped Siena's hand. "I thought never to see you again, milady."

"Where is the rest of your staff?"

"In the larder, milady. They will be back shortly."

"Elsa, no one must know that you have seen me. It's dangerous for both of us. I've come to rescue Michael. We will need some food for the trip back to his home."

"Thank the heavens, someone is going to free that poor child. He has suffered here." She grabbed Siena's arm. "But it will be impossible for you to escape."

"We'll take our chances. His father should be meeting us on the way back home, and then he will be safe. Now go and gather a bit of food and put it in a sack so no one knows that you've helped me."

Elsa scurried around the kitchen gathering bread and cheese. "I wish you luck, milady. Your father has been in a towering temper since your brother was killed. If he finds you, it will not go well."

Siena hugged Elsa. "My father has been in a bad mood all his life. I must hurry. Remember you haven't seen me. Stay safe."

She dashed back to Michael's room. He smiled the minute he saw her again and she realized he'd thought she wasn't coming back for him. The child had had so much heartbreak at his young age that it broke her heart.

"I thought ye'd left me," he said in his small Scottish voice.

She gave him a big hug. "I'm not going anywhere without you, I promise. Let's make this bed look like you're still in it."

"Why?"

Because we want to make it look like you are sleeping if someone comes into your room to check on you."

Siena put a pillow under the covers and bunched the blankets around the pillow to make it look like a small child was asleep.

"Wait," Michael said. He put his stuff rabbit beside the pillow.

"Are you sure?" Siena asked.

"I'm a big boy now. I won't need my rabbit or blanket."

"Yes, you are a big boy. But your rabbit wasn't here before so I really think you should take him."

Michael smiled and tucked him under his coat.

She moved the chest, then pressed the secret panel so the door would open. She looked at Michael before they entered the tunnel and said, "It will be dark for a few minutes, but there is a torch."

He nodded his head but gripped her hand tightly.

Thank goodness the torch hadn't gone out. Siena shut the door while she pictured the chest moving back into place. She listened and sure enough, she could hear the scrapping as the chest settled back in place. Agatha had told her that Siena's mother had had the passageway made without telling her father in case she needed to escape. Evidently, her mother had had doubts about her father, too.

"It's dark," Michael whimpered.

"I know, but we'll be outside soon." She held the lit torch but it barely cast a glow on the steps leading down to the tunnel so she could see why he was afraid.

"I'm afraid of the dark, but I'm a big boy now so I shouldn't be afraid," he said as he clutched her hand harder.

"Even big boys are afraid sometimes," she said, trying to address his worries.

"I have an idea," she said.

"Stars above
Stars are bright
Light this tunnel for us tonight."

TINY FLECKS OF LIGHT HUNG IN THE AIR LIKE LIGHTNING BUGS. IT was as if they had their own stars to guide them. Now they could see ahead of them.

"How did you do that?" Michael said in awe.

"It's magic." Siena smiled. "Now, we must hurry, however, these steps might be slick since it's so damp in here, so I want you to be very careful not to fall. Hang on to the back of my cloak."

She went first and Michael followed her. He slipped once

but she caught him, and he giggled. She was glad he was no longer afraid. When they came to the long hallway, he grabbed her hand and they made their way to the very end of the tunnel.

Once they were outside, they had to wait a few minutes for their eyes to adjust to the light. It was late in the day but still much brighter than the tunnel. At this time of the year, the days became longer.

Siena checked to make sure there were no guards, then she and Michael ran for the trees.

"Barra!" Siena called.

"Who is Barra?"

"A friend. You will see in a few minutes."

"I'm over here . . . come deeper into the woods," Barra said.

And sure enough there she was fluttering beside a horse.

"It's a fairy."

"She is. Barra is our friend."

"But nobody can see fairies."

"You have to be special to see a fairy," Barra said in her lyrical voice. "We must hurry, Michael. I could only find one horse, but I think it might be better this way."

Siena helped Michael up first and then she mounted behind him.

"It's best if we cut through the woods and stay off the main road until we are away from the castle," Barra suggested. "I'll cut a path for you. Follow me."

Siena smiled. "You know it is nice to have a fairy for a friend."

AFTER THEY HAD RIDDEN FOR WHAT SEEMED LIKE HOURS, SIENA felt like they would be safe to stop and rest. It was getting dark and she didn't think that they would find out Michael was missing until the next morning, which would give them a little time.

"Let's stop for tonight. I don't want to injure the horse. We can start again at daybreak."

She dismounted and then helped Michael down. "Let's get some rest."

"But it's so dark," Michael said, then added, "I'm not afraid anymore but it is still hard to see."

"I will build you a fairy fire that will keep you warm," Barra said as she swung her arm and pointed at the ground. A bluish light burst into a ball and hung just above the ground.

Michael gasped. "Someone will see."

"Nay, lad. We are the only ones who will be able to see the fire so we will be safe for a time."

"I wish I could do that," Michael said in awe.

Siena and Barra laughed.

Siena spread blankets on the ground and then she settled in with Michael. He curled up beside her and murmured, "I miss my, da."

Siena hugged the child. "He will be so glad to see you because he feared he never would." She stared at the magical fire which was very relaxing as they ate their bread and cheese. "How did the knights find you?"

Michael bowed his head. "I didn't stay in the cave as you told me to. I was afraid of the dark and I wanted my mother. So, I started down the hill and the knights found me and told me my mother was dead." He let out a little sob. "Then they put a cloth bag over my head, and I don't remember anything until I woke up in that castle room."

"It must have been very scary for you."

"It was, but I knew my da would find me."

"He thought that you were at Berwick Castle, my brother's castle so he attacked but you were not there. However, he never gave up hope and soon you will see him, and all this will be over."

Michael yawned, then asked, "Are you my mother now?"

Siena smiled. "I am. Your father and I are married. I hope you approve."

He snuggled next to her and said, "I like you."

As she shut her eyes, she prayed that Roderick would arrive tomorrow to keep them safe. Then everything would be perfect.

"THEY ARE COMING!" BARRA WAS FLYING ALL AROUND distracted.

Michael sat straight up. "What are we going to do?"

Siena thought for a moment. "I'm going to go back, and you will continue on with Barra."

Michael threw his arms around her neck. "Don't leave me."

Siena patted him on his back then pushed him away. "Listen, you must be brave, Michael. Barra will stay with you until you meet up with your father."

"What will happen to you?"

"I'm not sure but I'd rather they have me than you." She gave him a small smile. "I have some knowledge that they want. I also have magic that I didn't have before, so I'm sure I will be fine. Don't worry."

She got to her feet and saddled the horse, then kissed Michael on the cheek and helped him mount the horse. She gave him the reins. "Hold them tight but don't pull back or the horse won't go. Follow the path," Siena paused. "Tell your father that I have kept my promise in giving him back his son. I know he will be thrilled." She smacked the horse on the rump to get it going.

Wiping away the tears, she watched Michael until she couldn't see him anymore. "Be safe, little one." Then she turned back and started walking the other direction back to the place she didn't want to be.

She'd been walking for about thirty minutes when her father and his knights burst onto the path. Her father jerked his mount to a halt twenty feet in front of her. "Hello daughter," Cinge sneered. "Where is the boy?"

"Gone."

Cinge turned to one of his men. "Go after the brat and then I'll have them both."

Two riders broke out of line and started around Siena. She turned and pointed toward the cliff, clutching her stones.

The knights' horses bumped into something that no one could see. The horses reared and tossed the men off their backs. "There is something here," one of the men yelled."

"Nonsense," Cinge said.

"They tell you the truth," Siena said.

"How so?"

"Well, father you were right all this time. I am a White Witch and have prevented them from going any further. The boy will never be in your hands again."

162

Cinge didn't believe his daughter so he trotted his mount over to where the two men had fallen and he too hit something he couldn't see, knocking him on his backside.

Siena laughed.

He stood and brushed off his clothes before mounting again.

"I always knew you were an evil child," Cinge said. "But you will not get away from me. Malcolm is waiting at the castle and you are going to take him to find the Holy Grail or I swear that I will send every man I have to kill Roderick and his son."

CHAPTER 17

The Elliots were riding across the field to meet Roderick and his brothers. When they were ten feet from the Scotts they stopped.

"Look at those Elliots sitting there in those ugly plaids. Dull red and black, they should be ashamed to call themselves Scots," Angus grumbled.

"Isn't their motto, Bravely and Justly?" Roderick asked.

"Justly, my arse."

Roderick knew this brother was irritated and would complain about anything at the moment. "You Elliots are a pain in the arse!" Roderick shouted.

"Well that could be a matter of opinion," Joseph Elliot said with a sly smile.

"Do ye deny taking six coos off my brother's land?"

"I do," Elliot answered. "Angus can no speak for himself? Had to bring big brother along to help?"

"Ye, son of a bitch." Angus spat, then started to move forward, but Roderick grabbed his arm.

"Scotts stick together," Roderick said. "And as laird when ye steal my brother's coos then ye take from the clan."

"I told you I dinna have yer coos."

Roderick turned to Galen who had just ridden up, "What did ye find?"

"Six Scott coos. Needless to say, the old mon lies."

Roderick turned back to Elliot. "Ye were sayin'?"

Elliot smirked. "Mayhap they meandered over here."

"A lot of men could die today because as my brother said, ye are a lying son of a bitch or you can gather the coos and return them, and we'll forget aboot it this time."

"How about I give ye some information concerning yer wife in exchange for three of the beasts."

Roderick moved so fast that Joseph Elliot didn't have time to respond. Roderick had slid from his horse and jerked Elliot off his own mount.

Suddenly, swords were drawn on both sides.

"I'm in no mood for yer nonsense," Roderick spat. "So ye better tell me what ye are talking about fast before I slit yer throat."

The Elliots were all shouting until Joseph signaled them to be quiet. "A—An English rider dared to cross our land two days ago. When we stopped him, he said he had a letter for Laird Scott, and he was cutting across our land to make for a shorter trip."

"And?"

"So, we stopped the mon and read the letter to make sure he wasn't lying."

"And?"

"Out of the goodness of our hearts, we let him cross our land, but we could have sent him back to England, and then you'd never have received yer message. And for that –" He gestured with this hand. "I ken we should call some kind of truce."

Roderick wasn't sure if Elliot was lying to save his sorry hide or telling the truth. Why would he be receiving a message from England? It didn't make sense. "Ye are trying my patience. What did the letter say?"

"Well, now that will cost ye those coos we want."

Roderick's temper exploded as he slammed his fist into Elliot's jaw, knocking him to the ground."

Elliot rubbed his jaw but didn't bother to get to his feet. "That willna get ye the information about yer son."

Roderick jerked Elliot up and shook him. "What are ye talking about? What about my son?"

The Elliots were all dismounting, preparing for a fight. The Scotts would be happy to oblige them.

"He can huv two coos, but you'd better tell us what ye know and quickly before blood is spilled here today," Angus said, hoping they wouldn't have to do battle. This message sounded very important and he wanted to hear it too.

"Baron Cinge has yer son and he wants to exchange him for yer wife. Now let go of me!" Elliot shoved Roderick in the chest. "Yer choking me."

Roderick did let Elliot go and for a moment Roderick couldn't move. His son … his son was alive. Thank God. Michael was alive. He wanted to rejoice but knew the boy was still in danger. Or was this a very bad joke?

Galen and Duncan came up behind Roderick and slapped him on the back. "The boy lives."

"I knew it even if my hope was slim," Roderick said.

"I'll send a couple of men home with the coos and we'll ride to get the boy," Angus said.

Roderick shook his head as he watched the Elliots leaving. "First we go home. If we show up without Siena, Cinge is likely to kill Michael."

"But ye'll no make the trade?" Galen asked.

"Of course not. But we will make him think that we are going to trade her for my son." Roderick headed for his mount. "We've no time to waste."

———

In no time they were back at Black Dawn and Roderick and his men were dismounting.

"Water and feed the horses, then rub them down. We'll be leaving in two hours," he instructed Garvin. The stableman nodded but didn't say anything as he took charge of the horses.

Roderick and his brothers made their way up the hill to the great hall. As soon as they entered the door, Roderick called for his steward. "Martin!"

Martin slid as he rounded the corner. "I dinna ken ye were back, sire. There was a message for ye while you were gone." He reached for the paper that had been left on the desk.

Roderick took the note, then said, "Tell my wife, I want to see her."

"She isn't here, sire."

"Where is she?"

"I dinna ken. I just know she is gone."

"Yer not making sense," Roderick's voice was cold and exact. "Find Agatha and tell her I want to see her now."

Roderick, Duncan, and his brothers walked over to the high table where the servants had sat out a tray of bread and cheese for them. Everyone sat down and grabbed some food as it had been a long time since they last ate.

Duncan said as he poured a cup of ale, "Where do ye suppose Lady Siena is?"

"I have no idea," Roderick said with a sigh. He took a bite of bread and then unfolded the note and read the words out loud to everyone. "At least Elliott told the truth so 'twill save me having to go back and end his miserable life."

"Probably the first time," his younger brother grumbled.

Just then Agatha came scurrying into the hall. "I told her not to go but she wouldn't listen."

Agatha was wringing her hands.

"Calm yerself, Agatha," Roderick said. He stood and placed a hand on her shoulder. "Where did Siena go?"

"To her fathers . . . the miserable cur."

Roderick felt like his head was about to explode and he was momentarily speechless. Finally, he gritted his teeth and asked, "Why?"

"S—She said she thought she could rescue Michael, then escape with the child without anyone finding out."

"She couldn't wait for me?" Roderick thundered.

Agatha stepped back.

"No need to shout at her," Duncan said, and he stood, too.

Roderick glared at him.

"I told her to wait," Agatha said, quickly. "But she didn't want any bloodshed or for you to have to decide between her and your son."

Roderick shook his head. "She has little faith in me. How long has she been gone?"

"Two days, sire."

Roderick glanced at Duncan. "Give the word that we ride in two hours."

THEY TRAVELED HARD UNTIL THE NIGHT CAME AND THEY WERE forced to stop and rest the horses.

Roderick couldn't sleep because all he could think of was Michael and Siena. He prayed that neither of them was hurt. When was she going to trust and obey him? She was only a woman and not capable of taking on her father and his men. That was his job. What if something happened to her? He paused and then shook his head. Damn, he just realized that Siena meant the world to him. He wasn't sure when it had happened, but he couldn't remember not having her in his life.

And his son... his prayers had been answered or would be once his son was in his arms again.

At the break of dawn, they were riding again. The ride was hard and fast-paced, but no one complained. They all knew what was at stake. It was noon when they spotted a lone rider . . . a very small lone rider.

"Michael," Roderick shouted and watched the child's head jerk up.

Michael looked up at Barra who was flying above him. "Is it really *da*?"

"It is. You have made it to safety, Michael. I'll leave you now and go back to the castle. Stay safe and go meet your father."

"Thank ye, Barra," Michael said, then kicked his horse in the sides. In no time, he was even with his father.

Roderick jerked the child from his horse and smothered him in a hug. "I dinna believe I've found ye. Are ye hurt, son?"

"Nay," Michael said as he leaned back with a big smile on his face. "Hello Angus, Galen, and Duncan"

"Lad, we thought we'd never see ye again," Galen said as he reached over and touched the boy on the shoulder.

"I dinna think so either."

"Look at ye," Angus said. "Appears ye've grown two inches, lad."

Michael threw out his chest, then said, "I'm a big boy now."

"Yes, ye are," Roderick said with a chuckle, then he asked. "Where is Lady Siena?"

"She saved me, *da*. Lady Siena came and took me out of the castle by a secret passage. She gave me this horse and told me to stay on the road until I found you."

"But where is she now?"

"She gave herself over to the bad men so I could escape. They are mean and will hurt her." Tears rolled down his face. "Ye have to save her."

Roderick frowned. A flicker of apprehension coursed through his blood. He would kill the bastards. For now, he managed to get his emotions under control as he asked,"Where did they go? "

"I dinna see, but I think they went back to that old castle."

Roderick gave the signal for everyone to dismount. Once he was on the ground, he took his son aside. "Can ye tell me where the secret passage is located?" Michael nodded and told him everything his father wanted to know.

"What are we going to do?" Galen asked.

"Michael, I want ye to return to Black Dawn with Galen."

"No, *da*. I dinna want to lose ye again." Michael wrapped his arms around his father's neck. "And Lady Siena – she said she is my mother. I dinna want to lose her either."

Roderick pried the lad's arm from around his neck. "Ye'll no lose me ever again, but I have to go and find Lady Siena, and I need to ken that ye are safe so that I dinna worry about you."

"Nobody will ever get ye again," Galen promised. "Ye can ride with me since ye are probably tired."

Roderick hugged his son once last time and told him he loved him. He felt something in the child's jacket. "What is this?" He reached in the jacket and pulled out a bunny.

"Lady Siena brought me my rabbit."

Roderick felt his throat closing and he had to clear his voice to say, "'Twas nice of Siena. Ye take care of yer rabbit." He placed Michael on Galen's horse.

"A word, Galen."

"Take five men and dinna let Michael out of yer sight for one minute until I return."

"He'll be in good hands."

"Something else, brother." Roderick leaned in and whispered something which made Galen nod, then smiled. "It's about time, brother."

Roderick and the rest of his men rode to Balan Castle.

Sometimes to get rid of evil it needed to be jerked out root and stem.

CHAPTER 18

They rode hard to Balan Castle but stopped at the edge of the forest just overlooking the castle.

"We stop here tonight," Roderick ordered. The men and horses needed to rest while he thought about his plan to rescue Siena.

He was going to give her a piece of his mind once he made sure she was once again safe. She should have waited for him. Instead, she put herself in grave danger. Then he said a prayer that she was safe, and she wouldn't object when he killed her father. The son of a bitch had held his son for a year. That thought made Roderick's hands shake. The man was responsible for injustice to his clan. They needed their revenge, too.

At the first light of day, Roderick took three men with him to find the secret passage Michael told him about. The rest of his men were to circle the castle and wait for them to open the main gate. No sense in getting some of his men killed breaching the walls when it could be avoided.

Michael had given good directions for finding the wall and warning him to take a flint with him to light the torch. In no time they were running down the torchlit tunnel knocking cobwebs out of their way as they climbed the stairs to the door. Roderick shoved on the door and the chest slipped enough so that they could get into the room.

Immediately Roderick saw his son's blanket, so this is where Michael had been held. Roderick bent over and picked up the blanket and tucked it in his belt. A cold fury seeped through his veins. The mon would pay, but for now, he needed to stay focused.

"Let us make our way to the front gate so our lads can come in an easy way." Luckily the castle's men were still sleeping and the guards at the gate were easily taken down with little noise.

The gate was opened, and the Scots swept into the court-yard and fanned out, but many stayed on the outside and surrounded the castle close enough to help if needed.

They were ready.

CINGE HAD JUST CRAWLED OUT OF HIS BED WHEN HE HEARD someone banging on his door. *Blast it was early*, he thought and then yelled, "Enter." He grabbed his pants and slipped them on.

David, his first in command, rushed into the room. "Milord, there are Scots in the courtyard! Laird Scott is there also."

"Kill them and be done with it."

"Milord, there are at least fifty Scots out there."

"So?"

"And a hundred more surrounding the castle. We are vastly outnumbered. Their laird said he was waiting on you."

Cinge didn't like hearing that small fact as he finished dressing. He grabbed his sword and made his way to the bailey. He would get rid of this Scot once and for all.

Once out there he scanned the courtyard. David hadn't lied. The Scots were everywhere, and their laird stood in the middle, feet braced apart, looking none too happy.

"Where is my wife?" Roderick yelled.

"My daughter is not here. She left yesterday with Lord Malcolm. I doubt you will ever see her again."

"Why is that?"

"She is taking Malcolm to the Holy Grail, and I'm sure he will kill her once she is no longer needed. My daughter is evil and has been since the day she was born."

"Ye are talking about my wife!" Roderick was seething. His temper was held by a slim thread of discipline. "And ye call yourself her father. Ye have never been a father to the lass. The only evil I see here is yerself, but I want ye to know before ye die that this is for Siena and for daring to hold my son captive for over a year."

Cinge's laugh rang harshly. "How is the boy?"

Roderick exploded as he shoved his sword in the air and shouted, "No mercy!"

It was a bloodbath. Roderick's highly trained warriors were far superior to the English soldiers. The Scots' swords whirled through the air and arms severed from their bodies now littered the ground.

Screams filled the air as Roderick advanced on Cinge. His knights tried to help protect Cinge but Duncan and Angus took care of them.

Roderick never took his gaze off his enemy until he met him. Their swords clanged metal on metal. They moved as if they were dancing... the dance of death. Cinge's face turned red with the effort of meeting Roderick's superior strength.

Finally, Roderick knocked the sword out of Cinge's hand and knocked him to his knees.

"An eye for an eye," Roderick spat.

Cinge glared up at Roderick. "You will never find her if you kill me. You will be too late."

"Ye will never know." Roderick thrust his sword through Cinge's black heart. As he withdrew his sword, he wiped the English blood off on the baron's clothes.

At long last revenge was his and he felt the burden he'd carried for so long lift from his body. However, without Siena, he could never be completely happy. She had somehow managed to become a part of him and he needed her. But how was he going to find her?

He watched servants as they filed out into the courtyard. He made his usual speech that Balan Castle was under his control and the servants wouldn't be hurt.

A stout woman who he assumed was the cook from her stained apron rushed over to him. "Milord, you are Lady Siena husband?"

"Aye."

"Lady Siena gave me a message for you should you come for her."

"And the message?"

"You must hurry. Go to Edinburgh and find the church of St. Stephens. Behind the church is a forest, and in the woods, you will find a small chapel hidden in the vines and that is where she will be if she survives."

"What is your name, lass?"

"Elsa, milord."

"Ye will be rewarded, Elsa, upon my return."

"I need no reward, sire. Just save milady. She is a good person."

"My thanks. How many men did she leave with?"

"Three, milord."

Roderick went to find Duncan.

"I'm going after Siena," Roderick told Duncan and his brother, Angus.

"Wait. We can send men with ye."

"Nay. I can travel faster by myself. This is something that I must do. I will meet ye back at Black Dawn."

CHAPTER 19

They journeyed along the tree-covered road with the only sounds being that of the horses' hoofs hitting the ground and the birds in the trees.

Siena was riding lead. So far, she had managed to keep their pace slow in hopes that Roderick would come after her. He'd saved her once before. Would he do so now?

However, on the second day, her hopes were dimming. Once he had his son back, he really didn't need her anymore. She felt that Roderick cared for her, but he'd never said that he loved her.

Now she had to think for herself and not depend on anyone rescuing her.

She was lucky that Lord Malcolm had chosen only two soldiers to ride with them for protection. What would happen once she led them to the Holy Grail? She wasn't sure.

She glanced back at Lord Malcolm. He hadn't missed many

meals. His middle was wide, his eyes were beady, reminding her of a big, fat rat that no one could trust. So far, he hadn't mistreated her, but she knew that he could tell his men to deal with her at any moment.

She had her magic but if she were too slow to react there was no telling what they could do to her. There was the possibility that she could disappear and be back at Black Dawn. That would be easy, but her father and Lord Malcolm would still seek to find her to satisfy their greed. Wasn't that the reason she was taking them to the Grail in the first place? She was protecting all the Scott clan, not wanting any of them to die for her.

Lord Malcolm rode up beside her. "How much farther?"

"I don't know. Perhaps midday tomorrow."

"Are you sure we are going the correct way? We are nearing Edinburgh."

"Aye. The place is a little past Edinburgh," she said glancing uneasily over her shoulder.

"The Scots are none too fond of us," Malcolm's voice, though quiet, had an ominous sound. "You haven't set a trap with your so-called husband? It would be a shame to have to kill him."

"I assure you that Roderick would be very hard to kill, however, my husband has no idea where I am, so you can ease your worries. Tell me, why is the Holy Grail important to you?"

"What a foolish question." Malcolm had a hard-cold-eyed smile. "It promises everlasting life and no man can ever conquer you, so I'll have all the power of any man living." Malcolm glanced around. "We have ridden far enough today. We'll make camp here tonight and tomorrow you had better fulfill your promise."

It was a long night with fitful sleep for Siena. She dreamed of her husband, wanting to see him and hold him. What if she never saw him again? Tears streamed down her cheeks at the very thought. She dozed off and on the rest of the night.

She needed a plan to get herself out of this mess.

THE NEXT DAY AROUND NOON, THEY ENTERED ROSLIN GLEN with its lush green foliage. They passed the old abandoned church, which was once grand, but no more as half of its walls had fallen.

As they rode past the structure, oak, elm, and ash trees surrounded them. The trees and ground had lots of flora, so they had to leave their horses behind to enter the forest.

"Why do we leave the horses?" one of the soldiers asked.

"Because the pathway we travel will be small and tangled with foliage. It will be easier and faster on foot. You two ..." Siena pointed to the knights. "You will have to clear the way with your swords or you could give me a sword and I can do it."

"Not a chance," Malcolm said.

The knights nodded and started to swing their blades to make a path through the woods.

The journey was a struggle and slowed their progress but finally, Siena heard a waterfall. Strange she was going to a place that she had never actually seen except in a vision, but she did remember in the vision the chapel was beautiful and she remembered there was a waterfall. They came out of the trees on the side of a beautiful waterfall that plunged sixty feet into a steep-sided gorge.

"Where in the hell are you leading us?" Malcolm spat and backhanded Siena.

Her hand went to her face to rub her stinging cheek. "If you hit me again you will be very sorry. You didn't expect the Grail would be easy to find, did you?" She looked at him as if he were stupid. "I've heard that men have searched for years and have never found the cup. You are close, but we can always turn back."

"No. I, too, have heard the tales," he admitted. "I chose not to believe in such nonsense." He looked around, then asked, "Now, where?"

Siena pointed up. "A small brown chapel should sit at the top of the falls. But first I need to get a stone out of my shoe before I can make the climb." She sat down on a small boulder to remove her shoe and shake the stone out. The soldiers and Malcolm were taking a drink from their pouches and not paying her any attention. She needed a plan.

Again, she prayed that Roderick would come for her. However, if he had any chance to find her, she needed to leave him some clues. How could he possibly know where she was going? She had relied on Elsa to give Roderick her message if she saw him, which meant that Roderick would have had to go to her father's castle. There was a possibility that might not have gone well.

She thought about what she needed to do and finally came up with a plan to leave something to mark her trail. Siena tore a couple of strips off her skirt and tied one to a branch beside her. It was the best she could do as she stood and said, "I'm ready."

The climb took her breath away and a couple of times she

stood aside so the men could pass her, giving her a chance to leave a couple more strips of her skirt.

When they reached the top, they could see on the other side of the river stood a small brown chapel covered in ivy which looked more like a cave than a church.

A small man came out of the door and stared at them but he said nothing. He was dressed in brown monk robes. His long, white beard came to the middle of his chest. He sucked in a breath and asked, "Why are you here?"

"These men seek the Holy Grail," Siena answered.

"Only the worthy can touch the Grail," the hermit said with raised brows. "First you must cross the stream."

Malcolm shoved one of his men in the back to go first. The soldier was halfway across the stream when he stepped on a slick rock. The current was so strong that he lost his footing and fell into the water which took him straight over the falls to his death.

"How are you supposed to get across the stream?" Malcolm asked.

"How indeed," the hermit said.

Malcolm shoved Siena to the edge of the riverbank.

Siena looked up at the hermit.

He smiled and said,

> Out of the darkening forest rode she.
> Over the waters so still.
> Down into the depths of her watery realm
> To wait for the moment death's knell.
> (Val Joice)

Siena looked at the water, which was anything but still. Her knees trembled. Crossing the stream looked impossible. Gathering her courage, she took a deep breath and murmured, "Be still." When the water had settled and remained calm, she pulled up her skirt and walked across the river never slipping once. As she turned around, she saw that Lord Malcolm had followed her. The minute her foot touched the riverbank, the water once again was swift.

"Charles, stay on that side until I come out," Malcolm ordered his soldier.

Siena strolled over to the hermit. "I am Lady Siena."

"I am, Nicene, keeper of the Holy Grail. I knew you would come someday."

"Where is it?" Malcolm shouted, shoving Siena out of the way.

Nicene let out a slow breath. "Inside the cave, milord."

Siena got to her feet, resisting the urge to curse Malcolm as she brushed off her cloak. She felt sure, he would get what was coming to him. There wasn't anything holy about the man.

Malcolm darted inside. He gasped. "There are many cups in here. How do I know which one is the Grail?"

"You must choose," Nicene said.

The gold cups glistened. Some had jewels, some were plain. Lord Malcolm looked at each one before he chose the largest cup of all. He picked it up and turned toward them.

"Is this the Grail?" Malcolm asked. "It's hot to the touch."

The cup glowed bright red and soon Malcolm was screaming as his body burned until he turned to dust. The wind swept into the chapel and picked up the dust, carrying it out and into the woods.

Siena gasped at what she had just seen.

"Lord Malcolm chose poorly."

EVEN THOUGH RODERICK WOULD RIDE THROUGH HIS OWN LAND to get to Edinburgh, he chose not to ride with his men so he could move faster.

After he crossed the Scottish border, he knew of many shortcuts that he could take to lessen the distance that he needed to travel.

He must get to Siena.

He rode hard but was forced to rest his mount when they came to a stream, however, he did not sleep and hadn't for two days. Urgency gave him the strength to keep going. The moon was full tonight and would light the way.

After his mount had rested, they rode through Edinburgh, then on to Roslin Glen, wondering how in the world he would find his wife.

He found St Stephens, the old church, that was partially destroyed. He rode around to the back where he saw four horses grazing. They had been hobbled so they would stay put, so this had to be the way to go, Roderick thought. He dismounted and left Hercules a good distance from the other horses so they wouldn't fight each other. "Ye stay here until I return," he told his horse who nudged his hand. Roderick gave Hercules a bit of grain to keep him happy while he was gone.

There was an opening in the foliage that might be the beginning of a path, he entered the lush green forest feeling a little helpless for the first time in his life. He knocked the undergrowth out of his way with his sword until he could see what looked like foliage that had been recently trampled and cut, a good sign.

Barra knew she was needed. After all, Laird Scott was her duty even if he didn't know that she existed, so she went to find him. And so, she found him traipsing through the woods but going the wrong way. He was swinging his sword to make a path.

Since he couldn't see her, she would have to give him a few nudges. Oops, he was turning wrong again. *Men had no sense of direction*, she thought. Barra bumped him beside his head and whispered, "wrong way." He turned back to his left and then looked behind him before he changed directions.

Roderick heard a waterfall and came to a dead stop when he found himself on the side of a cliff with a sheer drop to the right. He felt like there was someone with him, but he couldn't see anyone.

Where in the world was his wife? He didn't see a chapel. "Blast!" he swore. "Now which way?"

He glanced around. A small slip of white material caught his eye. After he retrieved the small piece of cloth, he felt like someone had bumped his head, so he looked around and then down. There was a small footprint in the dirt. Siena had left him a sign. There also appeared to be a small single path leading straight up.

"So, we climb," he said with a sigh, moving forward.

"Yes," Barra whispered.

He found Siena's cloth ribbons along the way, so he knew he was going in the right direction.

It was a tedious climb. Finally, when he reached the top of the cliff, he saw a knight sitting on a rock staring across the river. He hadn't noticed Roderick until he said, 'Where is she?"

The knight grabbed his sword and swung around. "Who goes there?"

"The Devil's Laird. I'm not in the best of moods, so I'd speak quickly if I were you."

Roderick saw the man swallow hard and jump back. His arm was shaking so badly that the sword was waving back and forth in the air. "I—I did not hurt the lady."

"'Tis good to know. Ye need not be scairt of me, then, but I need to know where my wife has gone."

"She and Lord Malcolm went into the chapel a short time ago. I heard screaming but no one has come back out. I cannot get across the river so I'm waiting."

"Ye may leave safely if you go now," Roderick said, then he moved closer to the stream which appeared to be knee-deep, but the water was swift. It didn't appear that he had much choice, so he stepped into the ice-cold water.

Barra flitted to sit on Roderick's shoulder. She held out her hand and said.

> Water swift as the morning light
> Be calm this day until the night.

IMMEDIATELY THE WATER CALMED SO RODERICK COULD WALK swiftly across. He really thought that was strange but didn't question his good fortune. Since he'd met Siena a lot of strange things had happened around him.

"My work here is done," Barra said in her little voice, she giggled and was gone.

Roderick turned because he thought he'd heard somebody laugh, but no one was there so he figured it was the wind and nothing more. However, deep down he felt someone had been with him since he entered the woods and he was grateful. Lord, he needed some sleep since he was now hearing things. He shook his head and ran the short distance to the chapel.

A golden glow showed through the doorway and a small monk stood inside the door with his back to Roderick.

Nicene watched as Siena reached for the chalice. Immediately, she was surrounded by the soft golden glow as she and the chalice rose into the air.

"What goes on here?" Roderick demanded.

Nicene turned to him. "Ah, I see you have come. Lady Siena wants to rid herself of the black mark on her arm. She feels she is evil, and she wants the magic of the chalice to remove the mark, but she also feels unloved and she worries that her husband hasn't come for her, so perhaps he doesn't love her. And she isn't sure she has much to live for."

"But I'm here now. And I do love her."

"Then you must convince her to come back before you lose her forever."

"No!" Roderick shouted. In three strides he was underneath where Siena floated in the air. He reached up and grabbed her ankle.

"Dinna leave me, lass," Roderick begged. "I need ye. Michael needs ye. I canna bear to live without ye." A tear slipped down his cheek and he knew it was the first time he'd cried since finding his wife dead and his son missing. "I love ye, Siena

"Please stay with me. Ye're not evil for if ye were you could never have touched the chalice." He pulled her down to where he could see her face.

Siena was drifting in such a peaceful place, and she was very content. The light was bright and warm as it welcomed her. But then she heard someone calling her name. Slowly, she turned and glanced down to see Roderick.

He had come. He was calling her. But did he want her? It sounded like it. She must return. As she drifted down, she heard the words she'd longed to hear ever since meeting the man. Roderick loved her. He really loved her.

The next thing she knew she was in his arms hugging him. "Wait," she said, and then she placed the Holy Grail back where she found it.

She turned and jumped back into Roderick's arms, kissing him with all the passion that burned in her soul. She heard his growl as he tightened his arms around her. The sweetness of his embrace intoxicated her. The smell of him--that masculine scent drove her crazy. His magnificent kisses were firm and demanding as he ruthlessly plundered her mouth, leaving her breathless. But they were still in a church and needed to come to their senses, so she pulled back.

"You came for me," Siena said with a smile.

"Of course, I came for you. Ye are my wife and I love you." Roderick looked around. "Where is Lord Malcolm? I have unfinished business with him."

"He chose poorly," Nicene said.

Siena had forgotten about the hermit. "I'm sorry. This is Laird Scott, my husband. And this is Nicene keeper of the Grail."

"I should hope so." The hermit laughed. "Since you have been kissing him."

Siena blushed.

Roderick nodded then repeated his question. "What do you mean he chose poorly?"

Siena answered. "Malcolm turned to dust when he touched the wrong cup. A gust of wind came in and carried the dust to who knows where."

Roderick's eyes widened as chills ran all over him. "That could have happened to you. Were ye crazy to take a chance like that?"

"But I chose wisely." She peeked down at her left arm and saw that her birthmark was still on her wrist, so she glanced at Nicene for answers. "Why?"

"You cannot change who you are, milady."

"But I wanted the mark gone."

"It is only a birthmark nothing more. It's time you accept who you are, Siena, and don't worry about what others think. There will always be naysayers. It's what you believe that matters."

"Nicene is a wise mon," Roderick said. "You are my wife, a healer, and will be the mother of my son. I wouldna want it any other way."

Siena nodded. From this day forward she would hold her head high and never worry again about what others thought. After all, she'd just learned she was a good person, or she would never have been able to hold the Holy Grail.

"Thank you, Nicene. I wish you well."

"Ah, milady, I'll be just fine, but I will have moved once again as others will seek the Grail and not for good reasons. Go forth and have a happy life, milady." Then the hermit turned to Roderick.

"Some can love more than once. It has taken you a while to realize the truth, laird." Nicene chuckled. "Remember this as I give you my blessings.

"True love is always worth working for because in the end 'tis the only thing that counts."

CHAPTER 20

*A*s they descended the steep path by the falls, Siena noticed Roderick had stumbled a couple of times, which wasn't like him at all.

"Are you all right?"

Roderick sighed. His back ached between the shoulders as if he'd been hit several times with a log. "Just a wee bit dizzy is all. I've no' slept in a couple of days." He pulled out his flask and took a sip, then offered it to Siena. "Once we reach Hercules, we'll make camp since 'tis late and then head for home tomorrow. I ken the danger is behind us now."

"That sounds wonderful as I'm tired also."

They finished their descent along the falls and then through the thick forest until they burst through the greenery to the setting sun.

Hercules snorted when he saw them emerge out of the dark green foliage. There were three other horses there also. Apparently, the knight only took his mount when he left.

A strong gust of wind blew around them. Siena could smell the rain that would be falling on them shortly. Thunder rumbled. "Why don't we stay in that abandoned church so we don't get soaked and you can get some rest. We can put the horses in there too for protection."

Parts of the roof were missing and there were holes in the walls but in several places, there was good shelter from the rain and wind. They unsaddled the horses and gave them some grain. An old bucket stood in the corner, so Siena used her magic to fill it with rainwater so the animals would have something to drink. Good thing all soldiers were trained to bring food for their mounts when they traveled, but Siena also produced some hay, so the horses would be comfortable. Roderick was too tired to ask where she got the hay from, and she was glad.

Siena set off to gather wood and branches so Roderick could start a fire in the fireplace that was thankfully not damaged. She had just gotten the last bundle in when the storm hit, and the rain fell out of the sky in sheets. Thank goodness the roof didn't leak where they were.

Roderick was having a hard time starting the fire until Siena nudged her pink stone which produced an instant blazing fire.

"Och, it started fast," Roderick said as he jumped back in surprise.

Even though it was spring, tonight would be cool. "Look in my bag, lass. There are a couple of bannocks and some cheese. 'Tisn't much but it will get us through tonight. Glad that I am that we have a bit of shelter tonight."

Siena placed the saddles so they could lean against them, then spread the blankets and tartans out in front of the fire. Next, she placed the food down and took her seat.

Roderick slipped off his boots. Then he grabbed a pouch from his saddle and offered Siena a drink while he settled himself. "Come, lean against my knee so I can see you while we talk."

Siena started coughing. "This is whisky. I was expecting water. I should know by now." She smiled. "I will say that the more I drink whisky the better I like it."

Roderick chuckled. "Fine Scottish whisky is smooth, lass." He waved an arm around. "What does this remind ye of?"

Siena tore off a chunk of bread. "The cave we stayed in months ago. That seems so long ago." She sighed. "Tell me about Michael."

Roderick smiled for the first time in two days. "My son followed yer instructions and met us on the road. I couldna believe it when I saw him. Thank you. Ye've made my life complete."

"And you have made mine." Siena smiled, then said, "I hope my father does not try anything else. It was the only reason I agreed to take Malcolm to the Grail. I didn't want any Scott to be hurt because of me."

"Lass, ye have little faith in me and that is one thing that needs to change, but you need not worry about yer father."

"What makes you think so?"

"An eye for an eye, Siena." Roderick's left eyebrow rose a fraction. "Your father was behind all the murderin' not mentioning keeping my son locked up for a year. That couldna have gone unpunished. We attacked the castle at dawn. Your father did have a fightin' chance against me. 'Twas a fair fight, but I killed him."

Siena swallowed hard; however, her eyes never left her

husband's gaze as she said, "He was never a father to me. Perhaps now we can live in peace."

"Och, I like the sound of that."

A flash of lightning streaked across the sky, just as Siena took another swig of whisky. She jumped and spilled whisky down her chin.

Roderick removed the pouch from her hand, then reached over and pulled Siena into his arms. "Here let me help you he said as he ran his tongue over her chin. "Ye taste good, wife." Her rose-red lips were definitely made for kissing, he thought.

Roderick caressed her earlobes with his lips, then pressed tender kisses down her neck. Siena shuddered beneath his subtle seduction. His lips produced a warm, tantalizing blush that covered her body with fever and created the most unusual yearning for something more. Her heart yearned for his touch and so did her body. She wanted to be held and protected in Roderick's arms. Hadn't she always wanted this?

Roderick pushed Siena back so he could pull his shirt over his head and rid himself of his kilt. Then he began removing her clothing, trailing his hands over her body. When he had removed her last garment, he threaded his fingers in her hair and said, "I love you." Slowly, his lips touched hers and devoured her with ravenous kisses, leaving her mouth burning with fire. She knew the flooding of uncontrollable joy.

A flash of lightning illuminated the glistening bodies of the two lovers as they came to know each other. Caressing, touching, sharing themselves as they never had with anyone else. Siena and Roderick were caught in their own whirlwind, seeking a release that only they could provide.

She slipped her hands around his neck, crowning in this new world of sensuality. Her breasts were crushed against

Roderick's chest. His dark, curling hairs rubbed the tips of her nipples into firm, taut peaks. Reaching up, she laced her fingers through his dark hair and pulled his lips to within her reach. She gazed deep into Roderick's mesmerizing eyes, finding a burning passion that she intended to quench.

His tongue plunged into her mouth, mating with hers. Soon their kisses matched the fury of the storm, becoming hotter and bolder as the fire between them built to a boiling point.

Roderick's hands glided along Siena's silky thighs before moving back to her ripe breasts. Trailing kisses down her neck, he lowered his head until he found her rose-tipped nipples, where he licked circles around the tight nubs. Her skin held the luster of creamy satin, and it felt smooth against him. He captured one trembling peak in his mouth, teasing it to the hardness of stone. She gasped as his other hand continued its path with agonizing slowness and found the tempting flesh she offered him. With a little coaxing, she parted her legs, and his fingers slid through the curls down to her moist warmth. God, she was tight. You would think that she was still a virgin, but he knew better. Groaning, he could wait no longer. His hunger consumed his self-control.

He had to have her—Now!

He flipped her over until he was on top. Spreading her legs further apart with his knee, he positioned himself above her and drove deep inside her warmth.

Slowly, he started to move, feeling her tightness surrounding his manhood. He shivered. She was driving him crazy with desire. He moved with the rhythm of love, building, driving, and finally consuming them both with a white heat that demanded satisfaction.

Siena cried out with fulfillment. Slowly, she floated back

down to earth on a cloud of contentment. Wrapped in the warmth of Roderick's arms, she felt a sense of peace. At long last, she felt safe.

"I love you, Roderick," she murmured just before she fell asleep.

―――――

FOR TWO DAYS THEY TRAVELED, ENJOYING EACH OTHER'S COMPANY and making mad passionate love at night. It was as if the rest of the world didn't exist.

On the third morning, Siena actually did feel like she was going home, and it was a nice feeling. She'd missed everyone.

"I have a surprise for you," Roderick said.

"What is it?"

"Ye'll have to wait and see."

They rode until the sun was almost setting. Finally, they were on the hill that overlooked Black Dawn just like when she first arrived at Roderick's home. But it was different.

"Oh my. Look!" Siena pointed. "It is no longer black," Siena said in amazement. She remembered the conversation they had a long time ago.

"Do you suppose that one day you'll paint the walls of Black Dawn white again?" Siena asked.

Roderick sighed. "One day when I can put the past completely behind me."

Siena gave him a small smile, hoping that one day the castle would once again be white and their awful past behind them.

· · ·

"DID YOU KNOW ABOUT THIS?"

"Aye." Roderick smiled, then said. "They have worked hard, my love, to restore the castle back to White Dawn. I ken it would please ye. The past is behind us and only good times lie ahead."

"Thank you," she said, leaning over to kiss him. "Let's go home."

When they rode through the gates people were cheering that their laird and lady were home once more. Standing on the steps of the great hall was everyone Siena loved.

Agatha was beaming, and Michael was jumping up and down waving. Elen was smoking her pipe and someone had brought her a chair since she was 105, but she was smiling, and Roderick's brothers were surrounded by their men who were cheering.

At last, Siena had found what she'd always wanted. A family who loved and wanted her.

Who could ask for more?

And if they didn't behave, then she had her magic stones and she'd simply turn them all into frogs.

THE STONES

I thought that everyone would like to see Lady Siena's magic stones that have been sitting on my desk while I wrote the book.

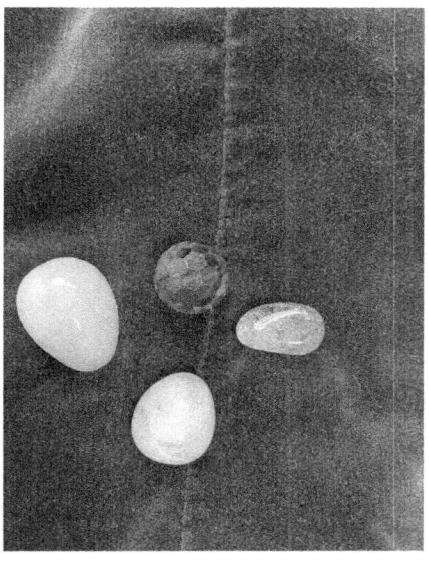

SNEAK PEEK

If you would like to see how a Scottish Lass handles a cowboy - look for SOUTHERN SEDUCTION on sale now.

Here is a sneak peek of the first chapter.

Texas Territory 1835

'Twas never good to lie . . . but sometimes necessary, Shannon McKinley reasoned.

Even if it was only a small lie . . . Well, in *her* eyes, 'twas small. Yet the farther Shannon traveled into this unknown land, the more she doubted her own sanity.

Suddenly, the stagecoach hit a rut, sending her and the other two passengers up to the roof and back down with resounding thuds. Shannon's bottom was now numb after two days of riding in this wooden crate.

She'd never dreamed the Texas Territory was so far away

from civilization. She'd been gazing out the window most of the day and hadn't seen anything that remotely resembled human life. Then again, perhaps, isolation was better for her because Mr. Griffin couldn't easily put her on a train if he was displeased that his mail-order nanny was much younger than what he'd advertised for.

Had it really been three weeks since she'd bid her cousin Jocelyn goodbye in New York? If Shannon closed her eyes, she could still picture Jocelyn and Brooke as the three of them stood by the rail of the ship, wondering what America would hold for them. Each of them had wanted their own adventure in America after leaving England. However, Shannon hadn't realized her adventure would take forever to begin.

The stagecoach hit another hole in the dirt road, but she didn't complain. What good would it do? However, she couldn't say the same about her two matronly traveling companions. They had complained constantly and were now threatening to lynch Shorty, their driver.

"I do believe Shorty has hit every blessed rock and hole in the road since we left Louisiana," Thelma complained as she straightened her sky-blue bonnet which kept slipping farther sideways with every bounce. "Why we have to ride in a mail coach is beyond me."

Emma glanced at her sister. "Possibly 'cause it's the only transportation into the Texas Territory other than on horseback and you, sister dear, have trouble walking, much less riding. You wouldn't last a mile on a horse."

"I'll have you know that I'm still younger than you, Emma dear," Thelma protested. "So don't you go getting uppity on me. I'd probably do just fine."

"You're only younger by two years. You'll be seventy before you know it. Remember, with age comes wisdom."

Shannon listened to the two elderly sisters bicker. She was growing accustomed to their bickering. It seemed to be what they liked to do best, and their presence most certainly had made the long trip much more bearable.

Thelma and Emma Miller were spinsters who lived with a third sister in Cottonwood. Together they ran the dry goods store. If these women were sixty-eight and seventy, Shannon wondered how old their other sister, Rose, was. However, if all the town's residents were as boisterous as these two, life would be very interesting in Cottonwood.

Shannon tried to make herself comfortable on the hard bench seat. If it hadn't been for the good sisters, she would've ended up wandering lost around St. Louis after she'd gotten off the train. She was looking for a coach similar to the ones they had back home -- something sleek and black with soft cushions instead of this hard wood. However, she'd quickly discovered the only way to get to the Texas Territory was by mail coach or horseback.

She glanced out the window. "Ye know, I ve not seen any sign o' life all day. Are ye sure somebody lives out here?"

Thelma chuckled. "This is the West, honey. The Texas Territory is just being settled, and we're probably lucky we ain't run into any Indians by now. You know, it's still a part of Mexico, not the United States. Still, the Americans outnumber the Mexican settlers now, and there's talk of independence."

"I huv tae admit I dinna know much about yer country. 'Tis my first time in America."

"You'll learn, dear," Thelma said, patting her knee.

Emma reached over and touched Shannon's hand. "Well,

we're mighty glad to have you," Emma said. "Don't hear many odd accents around here. Where did you say you're from, dear?"

Shannon smiled at Emma before answering. "Scotland," she said proudly, appreciating the woman's motherly ways.

"Do you have family in Cottonwood?" Emma asked.

"No. I've accepted a job tae be the nanny fer Mr. Griffin's children."

"The Griffin children," both women said at the same time.

Shannon nodded.

Thelma and Emma exchanged wide-eyed looks. "You poor thing," Thelma said.

"Why do ye say that?"

Thelma shook her head. "Those youngsters are a handful."

"Their ma died two years ago, poor things," Emma added. "And since then they have been through six nannies."

"Interesting," Shannon said. She'd been a little concerned when the women had given each other funny looks, but what children were not a handful? "I'm sure 'tis hard on them without their mother."

"It is," Thelma agreed with a nod. "Their father could be the problem, though. You see, Luke loved his wife very much. Never seen a man so dedicated. He still mourns Ruth."

"'Tis perfectly common tae mourn a loved one."

"Don't know of any man mourning for two years." Thelma arched her fine brow. "Especially with young'uns."

Emma shifted and glanced quickly around as if someone were eavesdropping on them. "Now, I'm not one to gossip, you understand." She paused and waited for Shannon to nod before proceeding. "I think Luke pushes his children away from him because they remind him of their mother."

"'Tis verra sad," Shannon murmured with a sorrowful shake

of her head. What would it be like to have a man love her like Mr. Griffin loved his wife? She sighed, figuring she'd never know.

Her da had told her more than once that no man would want someone who was as homely as she was. Especially with her god-awful red hair. Shannon pushed his words away and concentrated on the present. "What happened tae their mother?"

"Ruth came from back East and was used to city life. She was too delicate to live in Texas and couldn't adjust to the harsh environment. Must say, she stayed sick all the time. And then one day, Ruth took to her bed and never got up again," Emma said with a sad shake of her head. "She was such a pretty little thing."

"Surprises me that Luke would hire you," Thelma interjected. "You're mighty small yourself."

"But I'm not frail," Shannon informed them.

They both raised their eyebrows in doubt.

"'Tis true. I'm a bit tougher than I appear." Shannon insisted with a defiant tilt of her chin.

Emma reached over and patted Shannon's knee again. "We sure hope so. However, if things get bad for you, you're welcome to come and stay with us for a spell. We like you."

Shannon smiled her thanks to the kind ladies, then turned to stare out the window. Just how bad could it get? she wondered. Were the children truly holy terrors?

Mr. Griffin's letter had said his children were adorable. Could he have lied just as she had lied to him?

"We'll be in Cottonwood in about an hour, ladies," Shorty shouted from up top. She was sure Shorty must have a last name, but since arriving in St. Louis, she heard many men referred to by some nickname or other. Nothing formal like she was used to, and she definitely hadn't heard any titles. It seemed no one here had one.

She remembered one man at the St. Louis post office was referred to as Rattlesnake. Shannon didn't want to know how he'd earned such a name. Just the sound of it made her shiver. She hated snakes.

She most certainly was going to make sure she didn't end up with a nickname. Several strangers had already called her Red because of her hair, which she hadn't appreciated at all.

She could be touchy about her hair. God must have given her this odd color for some reason, but she'd yet to figure out why.

Just another hour, Shannon thought with relief, then she could get out of these cramped quarters. She turned back to the window and gazed at the countryside. The land wasn't exactly what she'd pictured. It was nothing like the beautiful, lush green hills in her Highlands. Instead, what she'd seen of Texas was brown and flat with few trees. And the dust . . . that was definitely something she would have to get used to. Even now, the temperatures were much warmer than she was accustomed to, and it was autumn. She wondered what summers were like in Texas if it was still hot.

Mr. Griffin had come to live in Texas from St. Louis, so he must have seen something promising in this land. What would Mr. Griffin be like? Pleasant, she hoped. From his letters and what the sisters had said, he sounded like a nice man who had cared for his wife. His penmanship had been beautiful, so she figured he was educated. However, she wasn't going to worry about Mr. Griffin for the moment. Shannon would do as she always had: face the problem head on once it presented itself. For all she knew, Emma and Thelma could be exaggerating.

Besides, if Shannon could handle men and their childish ways, she was sure she could handle one heartbroken rancher and his children. Two children shouldn't be that difficult.

Strange, she thought, she was traveling through hostile land, yet she felt safe. Way out here, her father would never be able to find her. And that was the way she wanted it. Just the thought of Angus McKinley made her shudder as though she were cold. 'Twas hard to believe that he was her da. He'd never shown her any kind of love. Just the opposite. He was a cruel mon.

Her mother had been English and her father was a Highlander, so, of course, the Highlands were where she'd grown up. Shannon couldn't say that she'd had a happy childhood. Most of it had been spent in fear of her drunken, domineering da. She could remember begging her mother to leave their home, but she had insisted that it was her duty to stay.

Angus was a mean drunk, bullying the weak and the small. Elizabeth, Shannon's mother, had tried to protect her from being beaten, and most of the time she'd been successful, hiding Shannon when Angus was in a foul mood.

However, the morning she'd found her mother lying cold and still at the foot of the stone stairs, Shannon knew her father had been responsible. He claimed he'd never touched Elizabeth, and maybe he hadn't, but she was still dead. He'd pointed out that her mother might have tripped on her gown and fallen during the night, but Shannon had seen the bruises on her mother's arms and around her neck, and she knew . . .

Shannon had felt guilty that her mother had suffered and she hadn't been able to help her. Perhaps, if she'd been with her mother, she could have pushed Angus away, and then he'd have been the one at the foot of the stairs.

Things had grown worse after her mother's death. When Shannon was alone with her da, she had endured the beatings her mother had protected her from. However, once she'd turned seventeen, something in her had snapped, and she'd warned her da that if he ever placed a hand on her again she would kill him.

He had simply laughed.

But she'd meant every word.

It didn't take long for Shannon to realize that Angus could easily kill *her* before she had a chance to defend herself. So she ran with the help of Douglas, one of her da's men, who'd enabled her escape to England. Later she learned that Douglas had been killed when Angus had discovered his ruse.

In England she'd found refuge with her uncle Jackson Montgomery, Duke of Devonshire. Jackson, her mother's brother, had been a good man.

"Why are you frowning so, dear?" Thelma asked.

Slowly, Shannon turned from the window. She felt dead inside when she thought of her da. "I was thinkin' about my home."

Emma shifted over to the other bench so she could sit beside Shannon. She slipped an arm around her shoulders. "It's only natural that you'll be homesick."

Shannon gave the women a small smile. There was little chance that she'd be homesick. Nonetheless, she remained mum. She didn't want to explain her past to women she barely knew.

"What the hell!" Shorty swore from up top.

Shannon glanced out the window. "Looks like a town up ahead."

The stage pulled to an abrupt stop, nearly throwing her from her seat. Dust swirled around the stage so thickly that Shannon had to jerk her head back inside to avoid a mouth full of grit.

Thelma peered out the window on her side. "I believe we're finally home," she said. "But I wonder why Shorty stopped way out here on the edge of town? The post office is down the road a ways."

They didn't have long to wonder because Shorty yanked open the door. "Ladies, appears there's a gunfight going on in town, so we better not get too close. Wouldn't want to see anybody hurt or nothing."

"A gunfight?" Thelma said, stepping out of the stage, followed by Emma, who added, "What in the world . . ."

"Ladies! Get back in the stage!" Shorty barked.

Well, Shannon surely wasn't going to stay in this stuffy box one minute longer than she had to, so she followed the ladies out the door.

Shorty grumbled and hastened alongside her.

Shannon's steps quickened. It appeared that her quest for excitement was already starting . . . a real live gunfight.

They moved down the boardwalk, careful not to get in danger's way, but close enough that they could see what was happening. Sure enough, two men were squaring off in the middle of the street and there was a crowd gathered on the boardwalks to watch.

The man whose back was to her was several inches taller than his opponent. He made a striking figure from behind. His shirt stretched across his broad shoulders and he was dressed all in black. Usually, the bad guy wore black, or so she'd read. This was certainly how she'd pictured a cowboy to look.

"I wonder why they are fightin'?" Shannon asked.

"Could be anything," Shorty answered. "Sometimes it's just the way a man looks at you."

Emma and Thelma strolled over to stand beside them. "This isn't the way we'd like to introduce you to our little town, but out here men and guns are plentiful, so I guess you'd best get used to it, honey."

"'Tis the same at home," Shannon said. "Only 'tis broad swords they use fer weapons." She glanced back at the combatants in the middle of the dusty dirt street. "After this is over, I'll huv tae send word tae Mr. Griffin that I've arrived."

Emma gave her a strange smile. "No need, honey."

Confused, Shannon turned to Emma. Something vaguely disturbing tugged at her, warning her that she wasn't going to like the answer to her next question. "Why?"

"Because Luke Griffin is the tall one out there." Emma nodded toward the street. "He's the one dressed in black."

Speechless, Shannon let her gaze wander over the man. She became aware of the tension and energy about his body that made her think of an animal ready to attack.

So this was her employer. Was the mon crazy? He could be killed and leave his children orphaned. He could be killed and she'd be without a job.

Then what would she do?

ABOUT THE AUTHOR

Brenda Jernigan is a bestselling author. Her books have been nominated for many awards - Book Seller's Best Award, The Maggie Award, and The Holt Medallion Award. Publishers Weekly said, "Brenda Jernigan writes Romance, Adventure and Magic."

She grew up living the life of a tomboy – climbing trees, playing ball, and excluding starry-eyed romance from her daily repertoire. Brenda discovered the love of books while taking her son to Story Hour at the local library -- she was hooked. She set an ambitious goal and began work on her first novel. She continued to write six more novels in rapid succession. She figured having the same birthday as Ernest Hemingway couldn't hurt.

She is a member of RWA, NINC, PAN, PASIC, and Outreach International Romance Writers where she was President.

Her books have been printed in several languages and her last book "Southern Seduction" written under the name of Alexandria Scott was printed in Russian.

If you have read and enjoyed the book, please leave a review on the vendor's webpage. Nothing sells books more than word of mouth. Thank you in advance for reading my books.

Follow me- below...

http://www.brendajbooks.com
https://www.goodreads.com/
goodreadscombrenda_jernigan
https://www.bookbub.com/profile/brenda-jernigan
https://www.facebook.com/bkjbooks
https://twitter.com/bkj1608
http://www.amazon.com/-/e/B001KI2LIK

ALSO BY BRENDA JERNIGAN

NEW RELEASE JANUARY 1, 2021

THE DEVIL'S LAIRD

Roderick, Warlord of Kirkurd is driven by revenge and guilt. When his holding was attacked, his wife ravished and slain, and his son lost to him, the goodness within Roderick died. Now he is known as the Devil's Laird. Revenge will be his.

The Ladies Series
THE DUKE'S LADY

LOVE ONLY ONCE

THE WICKED LADY

CHRISTMAS IN CAMELOT

The Misfit Series
DANCE ON THE WIND

UNTIL SEPTEMBER

WHISPERS ON THE WIND

SEPTEMBER STORM

THE CHOICE

BLACK MAGIC

DIAMOND IN THE ROUGH

THE MISFITS

STORMY PASSION

SOUTHERN SEDUCTION

WESTERN SEDUCTION

e-mail - bkj1608@juno.com

webpage -www.brendajbooks.com

Follow me on Twitter - @bkj1608

Printed in Dunstable, United Kingdom